IN THE BEGINNING

Nick Girard

ISBN-13: 978-1-0922-9042-5

For Cake

The Old Testament

Chapter 1

God

In the beginning there was only God and the infinite space of existence, which was Heaven. God was a sphere of magnificent white brilliant light, a globe of radiating electrified energy that was... alive. God's light was an intensely dazzling and magnificent powerful force, destined to command respect and authority. It filled all of the Heavens with its brightness and nothing was absent of its greatness. God floated throughout Heaven, visibly beating like a heart, pulsing with glowing white energy that bolted and charged from within. Currents of power rippled across God's surface, the energy moving with each thought and emotion.

Dominating and commanding an unwavering level of superior control over existence was God's fundamental purpose. An unchallenged being with a defined essence of absolute power and great perfection.

God alone had the ability to generate matter from nothing and decided it was necessary to create subjects to rule over. Heaven's infinite space would now be populated by these servants who would live to worship the divine Almighty as the first creations in existence.

Chapter 2

Angels

God created one thousand Angels.

The Angels were gaunt spindly beings with faint silver almost translucent skin. They were long lean characters with a physical nature that did not resemble strength in appearance. Angels had no gender and their bodies were all identical in height, length, and diameter. The only characteristic that was specific and defining to the Angels was the structure and color of their faces. Each Angel's face had a different color and configuration, which distinguished them from one another. The colors varied in brightness and included all the different spectrums of light. The facial symmetry of the eyes, mouth, cheeks, chin, and ears were all quite distinct and gave each a stunning originality.

Each Angel was also given a gift from God. A piece of God's light was placed in the very center of each Angel's chest and the light softly glowed red, lighting up the core of their bodies. The soft light extended through their nearly transparent limbs and softly shone through the veins that ran through them. The red light beat and pumped the energy of God throughout their figures and was the source that powered their existence. It was a way of reminding the Angels that they were God's creation and the only reason they could live.

Each Angel also had a second gift from God and that was the gift of flight. All of God's Angels were bestowed with a pair of wings so they could fly throughout Heaven wherever God required them to go.

The wings of an Angel were strong, thick, massive, streamlined pieces of beauty that rested on their backs. These impressive stark white lustrous feathered wings compensated for the Angel's lack of physical strength in appearance. The sight of an Angel with wings spread was an amazing majestic display. The wings were twice as long as an Angel's body when fully extended. When not in use, the wings were drawn in, folded close to their form in an elegant and neat fashion with the tip of the wings bend resting at least four feet above their heads. Their flight defied the laws of physics and a single flap would propel them at astonishing speeds over a tremendous distance. They could even hover for a continued length of time with only one beat from these mighty wings.

As God floated throughout Heaven, the Angels would always follow. Never flying at the same level as God but always carefully behind and underneath. No Angel could be on the same level as their master, no one was worthy of that.

The Angels were all created equal and God had purposefully designed them to have similar character traits and personalities. In order to have control over the Angels, God needed them to share the same form of behavior. They were easily influenced and at this time lacked the ability to have any real original thought. The Angels all acted as one with God's guidance and were not able to think for themselves but instead acted as a collective unit under God's advisement. They were emotionally fragile, volatile, and impressionable creatures. These characteristics were the ideal traits necessary to exhibit full control over another. None of them questioned their leader and all wanted the same thing, to be closer to God.

At this time Heaven was only a white infinite space that was extraordinarily bright from God's white light. The Angels traveled in a submissive flock throughout Heaven, always trailing their creator with their glowing beating red bodies. God led them throughout Heaven and they desired nothing more than to be close to their maker at all times.

Chapter 3

Love

Love is a pure and unconditional care for another. If you have true love then everything else in life becomes meaningless. One becomes willing to sacrifice everything in order to protect the one they love and one's willingness to perform an action that once seemed incomprehensible is now thought to be justified. It gives one the security of trust. A trust so secure that it instills a subconscious confidence in the ability of the one you love. A conviction of knowing that no matter what the circumstance, the being that loves you will always come to your aid. If nothing in your life existed except for the one you love then you would be fully content. There is nothing in existence that challenges it nor anything that can come between it.

God, being the ultimate power in Heaven, dominated everything and ruled with an unwavering level of control. If all the Angels chose to do God's bidding without question they would then be rewarded.

The reward came in the form of God's love, which was

the only desire of every Angel. Love was an emotion God invented and since God was the creator of love it meant that God could manipulate it. The desire for God's love was everything to the Angels and they did not have the ability to love anything else.

Chapter 4

Worship

Angels were required to constantly proclaim their love for God. The Angels expressed their devotion through relentless prayer and this was called worship. God demanded worship and praise and these mandates were described in Heaven as the "Will of God." This "Will of God," was never to be questioned or challenged and was of the utmost importance. To be worthy of God's love required the Angels to follow God blindly and to never question any demand that was made.

God decided it was necessary to test the Angels' level of devotion and commitment by introducing doubt.

The actions and decisions that God performed would now be allowed to be questioned by the Angels. This doubt in God's ability resulted in fear, fear for the looming punishment that God would distribute should the doubt limit the amount of worship that an Angel was required to perform.

If the doubt was not eliminated, God would then punish

the Angels by denying the love once bestowed upon them, maliciously rejecting them. God would banish the disgraced Angels to the far reaches of Heaven in order to isolate them from the sanctity and solace of the collective.

The isolated Angels suffered greatly by God's actions and became terribly distraught and panic-stricken with the situation. They only desired to be welcomed back into the good graces of God and to be loved again. They would pray and worship with such intensity that it would drive them to a state of exhaustion where they would become almost catatonic. Only then would they be welcomed back into God's embrace with God demanding they ask for forgiveness.

Chapter 5

Forgiveness

Once an Angel admitted their lack of devotion and doubt, God would then allow forgiveness for what was called a sin. A sin was any act that brought attention away from praising and worshiping God.

God used forgiveness of sin as another tool of control. Angels believed that their flaws and mistakes could be accepted if they only asked for forgiveness. Once God granted forgiveness they would then be showered with love. The emotion felt after being forgiven was electrifyingly powerful and rejuvenated the Angel's purpose in existence. It confirmed their continued belief that God was a great, kind, and loving being. Even God could be humble enough to forgive their unworthiness.

The construction of the hierarchal foundation of Heaven was complete. God had secured dominance over the Angels by controlling love, worship, doubt, fear, and forgiveness. The desire of God's love was the only purpose of an Angel and proved to them that God was their master.

Chapter 6

The Design of Heaven

God decided it was time to transform Heaven into a place that represented the ferocity of what it meant to be the all-powerful being that ruled existence. The environment of Heaven would now adapt to God's different emotions. Heaven would be a calm tranquility when God was content, and furiously violent when God was angry.

The atmosphere of Heaven became breathlessly cold and crisp and had a sharp strong wind that blew relentlessly throughout its eternity. The sky of Heaven became a pale infinite ocean of blue that was continuously occupied by fantastically massive roiling clouds that churned endlessly into ever-changing shapes. They billowed in and out of each other and God's light shone through them, spilling out of one cloud and into the next in a commanding striking dance. The clouds foreshadowed the sentiment of God and flowed together like a smooth sea of wisping fog in times of prolonged worship performed by the Angels. When the Angels suffered from doubt and lacked devotion the clouds became intense, contorting themselves into huge masses that looked like misshapen boulders rolling through each other in a violent show of God's emotion.

The wind in Heaven began to transform. It blew with a harsh severity, and like the clouds, it behaved in the current environment that Heaven was in. Cruel and powerful winds were created that would turn into sweeping tornadoes that swerved and bent, lashing across the Heavens. The wind cut deeply into the Angels and made them feel helpless and at the mercy of the force of God. There would be hundreds of ferocious cyclones changing colors from dark to light as they whipped throughout Heaven. It was an amazing and horrifying sight that immediately made every Angel appreciate the raw power behind them. The tornadoes would strike them with terrific fear and awe at the same time. It put them in their place knowing that God could create such a terrific and breathtaking event. They knew that it was their doing that caused this aggressive display of the elements and they immediately redoubled their level of worship with the hope that God would forgive them and stop the vicious assault on their environment.

With Heaven's elemental domain functioning, God now focused on creating its foundation, a pure white seamless marble floor. It was solid and severely cold to the touch with an end that could not be seen. The surface was a continuous sheet of impeccable perfection. It was an unyielding base that provided the Angels with a feeling of safety. There was security knowing that God had given them this resilient ground to their domain. The marble was thriving and behaved like a mirror that swirled with the reflection of the clouds, constantly morphing its reflection with the changing sky above. The image of the marble was clean, stark, and beautiful. This represented the integrity of Heaven.

There was another form that existed on the marble. It was a fine white sand that swirled and spun throughout Heaven like an ocean. It created great massive mounds and huge dunes on the infinite floor. The sand was very fine and each piece was a sphere; a grainy globe of small white stone. The pieces of sand churned around Heaven's atmosphere and created what looked like a floating fog on the marble floor. It gave the effect of walking on air and symbolized the spirit of God; it was all around you at all times. It was the touch of God when God was not there, a force that was also an object, always with you and always a part of your life.

This sand gave the Angels comfort but also fear. They loved the pure white sand in times of calm and peace. The sand was as soft as silk when underfoot and provided a soothing restful blanket of contentment. It absorbed the echo of Heaven's infinite expanse and relaxed the Angels as they lay casually in the natural dunes it created. But when Heaven's tranquility was broken by God's anger the wind would hurtle the sand into great storms, enveloping Heaven in a swirling stinging assault. The sandstorms ferociously spread like a thundering cloud that engrossed and shrouded Heaven as it rolled and billowed across the floor in a colossal cloaking tempest. It would block out all light and force the Angels to kneel on the ground with bowed heads in order to avoid the assault of the fine grain cutting across their faces. This was a method God used to force worship upon the Angels. Peace in Heaven would only be restored when God was content with the amount of praise being conducted. Fear of the storm caused the Angels to pray tirelessly and only when enough time had passed and God felt fulfilled would there be an end to the onslaught of the massive storm. As the wind died down and the sand rested on Heaven's floor the Angels would collapse with exhaustion. They laid trembling and scattered across Heaven in disordered masses as they recovered from the strain of enduring the wrath of God.

The Angels did not have the ability to completely control their consciousness. This caused brief lapses in their worship and doubt in their creator. God could sense the doubt and interruption of prayer amongst the Angels and would send the serene ambiance of Heaven's elements into turmoil, an end to the calmness as punishment.

Proper love and worship supplied by the Angels would result in God supplying a soothing and serene environment in Heaven. This tranquility immediately rejuvenated the love that the Angels felt for God and invigorated their energy to pray. God obviously knew this and enjoyed the added worship and love. A perfectly calm Heaven would be supplied in these cases. There would not be the slightest vibration, the clouds would stop moving, and Heaven would be as silent as a mirror as it reflected the pure happiness of the silence around it. When the Angels became exhausted from their relentless adoration and could pray no more, God would upend the harmony of Heaven and release a fury of tornadoes and rolling clouds in a vicious bombardment of emotion.

God enjoyed the fear and resultant torment it created, loving the additional worship that it supplied. But God wanted more. In order to be truly feared there needed to be something that would instantly command attention and stop a being from thinking. There needed to be an event so fantastic that it would inhibit the ability to focus and immediately summon a ferocious terror. God's movements, voice, and anger needed to be unavoidable. The most terrifying features in Heaven were created that would command ultimate attention, thunder and lightning.

Thunder exploded with an unheard of level of intensity throughout Heaven. It was as if the forceful sound had the ability to tear Heaven apart. It clapped again, and again, shaking all of Heaven to an immediate halt. The marble floor of Heaven shuddered beneath the feet of the Angels and the air literally moved due to the power of the formidable thunder. Nothing could escape the force of volume it created, the fear of enduring God's wrath. This made the Angels question their level of devoutness and gave them the immediate desire to pray and worship.

As terrifying as thunder was, there still needed to be another method that would command instant fear, this was lightning. It was a flash of brilliant striking heat that exploded in bolts across the Heavens. Darting through the sky and striking Heaven's floor it was paired with claps of thunder each time it struck. It was so bright and vivid that it instantly left every Angel temporarily blinded. The heat and energy was so severe that it caused your inner being to churn and gave the feeling that you may explode with intensity. It burned throughout all of Heaven like a sharp white-hot jagged sword. It tore through your thoughts and crippled any doubt you ever had about God's dominance. It literally electrified your being which was now rigid from the force of it.

These searing, painful, torturous forces were tools of control. God was a master of fear and power. When pleased, God would tantalize the Angels with tranquility and shower them with love and affection. When displeased, God would engulf the Heavens with a perfect storm of the elements. Wind, thunder, and lightning would torment Heaven and show how the creator of existence reigned supreme over everything.

God was absolute and cherished the ability to strike fear into the pure simplicity of the Angels. Fear of God made the Angels constantly long to earn love through worship and praise, which would ultimately bring them peace if done continuously.

Chapter 7

God's Kingdom

God needed a kingdom and commanded the Angels to build the perfect empire that was worthy of Heaven's greatness. It was to be an imposing majestic house of worship, a magnificent structure that would evoke awe and humble all that viewed the astounding domain.

God corralled the spinning tornadoes of Heaven into a churning circle and together they pulled in the massive quantities of Heaven's sand until a mound that reached the sky had formed. It was so tall that it almost touched the clouds. The wind stopped and God struck the mass with a thick bolt of lighting, belting the top of the immense mountain of sand, which sent a ray of heat straight through to the bottom. The mountainous dune glowed red and then the top exploded with a shower of bright crimson molten lava that quickly flowed over the tower of sand, covering every inch of it with the scorching flaming substance. Once engulfed in the red lava, the explosions ceased and the steaming fiery liquid cooled to form a massive stone mountain that brushed the sky. This would be the foundation of God's palace to be shaped by the Angels into a house worthy of God's significance.

Building the temple was now the only form of acceptable worship. No Angel was exempt from their duty and they were to use all ounces of their strength to construct the spectacular house. The Angels shaped the rugged mountain without the aid of tools. Using their hands they smoothed and carved the rock with the white sand from the marble floor, forming a pillared round temple at the mountaintop. It became a huge menacing structure. A great coliseum that shone white from the constant shaping the Angels performed using the sands of Heaven. The stone columns were immensely wide and so tall they appeared to not have an end. Each glistened like white ivory steel in the light of Heaven. Enormously cold and sturdy the coliseum was a prominent structure. Gleaming white steps were carved into the mountain and led from its base straight to the top in an almost vertical ascent. It would be a grueling difficult path to reach God's great presence. Once the stairs and columns were complete, a great room with no ceiling was polished within. The surface was solid and resembled a silverish stormy pool, reflecting the clouds and swelling storms that blew throughout Heaven. This is where the Angels would kneel before God in worship.

And now God created a throne. A wide crystal base formed on the mirror-like floor near the back of the temple and shot up to the sky in a tapered sparkling spike. At the top of the throne, God chose to preside and oversee the Angels. God would no longer lead the Angels throughout Heaven but would instead conduct their realm from the highest point in existence. The Angels would have to shield their eyes at the brightness of their master and strain themselves just to get a glimpse of the throne. The house of God was complete and now all would gather to honor their master.

God took a piece of the mountain and formed a dark

rustic stone bell that would hover just below the top of the throne. The toll of this bell was the creation of a sound unlike anything the Angels had heard before. It rang out like a shock wave throughout Heaven. The sound radiated through their bodies in a wave of force, a command to come to God. It's tolling turned the heads of all the Angels as they stood at the bottom of the stairway to God, fearing what would come next.

They then began to climb the steps to God's house, which was an arduous emotional task by design. The trek to the top was painfully hard and none were allowed to take flight to the temple. Thc bell tolled the entire time the Angels walked the steps and they traveled in fear of what was to come. Were they to be punished or rewarded? A terrible sense of anxiety filled them as they continued the trip to either feel the wrath or love from their master.

Chapter 8

The Sacrifice

The Angels gathered on the great floor and the bell stopped ringing as they all kneeled in silent even rows at the foot of the throne. Their great wings laid elegantly behind them as they kneeled, draping the ground in plush white feathers. The light of God shone brightly into their eyes and forced them to bow their heads. Once all had kneeled God let the silence drag on, torturing the already anxious Angels.

God believed in sacrifice and this worship would not end until one was made. The silence was broken after an agonizing wait with a breath of thunder that cracked the sky and vibrated off the mirrored floor. In the great room of the kingdom the sound echoed off the walls and floor with such force that it physically moved the Angels, making them tremble and shudder with the sound.

God spoke:

"I love all of you and I have never given you a reason to doubt me. And yet some of you choose to do so. Some of you do not worship me enough, some do not praise me enough, why does this happen? Without me there is nothing, I am the reason you exist and there is nothing in Heaven equal to my power. I can banish all of you from this paradise. I can give you pain and suffering beyond anything you have ever felt!"

The Angels were shuddering uncontrollably as God's voice became sterner and louder.

"Who here does not believe how great I am, who here does not believe in my power, that I am the meaning of existence?!"

God let the power of silence do the work again as the Angels continued to tremble in fear.

In this first day in God's house of prayer the Angels felt more fear than ever before. They were all guilty of sin for each Angel had internally questioned why they had been forced to build this massive house of worship.

Didn't they already praise and love God? Why did they need to construct something that seemed unnecessary? Why now did they need to add anxiety to their lives by climbing these steps in order to worship? Each Angel was quivering with dread as they separately knew that God was aware of the questioning thoughts that they shared.

God, of course, knew the doubt existed and chose to use this event as a way to test the subjects of Heaven. This uncertainty would be preyed upon and the Angels would be disciplined for it.

There was no movement from the Angels whose heads were still bowed in worship but now also in shame for the sins they had committed.

"Who will admit they have sinned!? All of you have doubted my kingdom and its purpose!"

The Heavens screamed and shook like never before as God rattled it with massive blows of thunder and shrieks of lightning that vaulted off the walls of the house. And then there emerged the first self-sacrifice, one Angel chose to take the fall for the rest and stepped forward.

All noise abruptly stopped as a dead calm settled over Heaven. The silence was unbearable and yet each Angel was relieved beyond expression that they would be spared. The Angels did not know how God would react to this new action of sacrifice that had never previously been performed.

God ordered the other Angels to stand and create two lines on the center of the floor with the sacrificial Angel standing in between and at the front of the newly formed ranks. The faulted Angel was then commanded to walk down the middle of the lines that had been formed. God's next command was for each Angel to strike the victim with the intent to cause physical pain.

This request confused the Angels for none of them knew how to harm another. This knowledge was not a part of their existence and they stood motionless in a paralyzed state of fear and perplexity.

They waited for another moment, which abruptly ended as God shouted:

"Attack!"

The first Angel in line struck the casualty squarely in the face with a closed fist. This was the first act of violence ever performed. Tears of sadness immediately began flowing down the faces of the aggressor and victim. They truly loved each other and were being torn apart by this action God was requiring them to do. They were all overcome by a great sadness since they couldn't bear the thought of hurting one of their own. However, deep down the Angels knew that God's request to attack had to be right.

The martyred Angel was beaten by the members of Heaven while moving through the gauntlet, each Angel sobbing uncontrollably upon completing the mandatory task. This action also came with a realization. The Angels had learned that they could inflict pain upon one another and that the pain affected them both physically and emotionally. The victim's face began to split open and a deep red liquid like substance that had never been seen before began to pour out.

It was blood, the blood that was pumped throughout their bodies from the light of God. The light was the beating force that thrust it through their veins. The savagery they were required to perform was draining the lifeblood out of one of their own.

The vast quantities of tears shed by the Angels began to accumulate and started streaming down the mountain in a great flood of water. When the suffering Angel was struck by the last member of Heaven God commanded them all to stop and abruptly dismissed them from the house of worship. The beaten Angel was ordered to stay behind and God bestowed a name to the voluntary self-sacrificed, Lucifer. It was the first Angel to be given an actual identity from the rest.

The other Angels raced away from the tragedy, sprinting down the steps in a blind emotionally distraught stampede. When they reached the bottom of Heaven's mountain they were met with a shocking surprise. The flood of tears which had cascaded down the steps did not pool on Heaven's floor but instead floated in the air above them, tinkling like suspended crystal raindrops and sparkling as if each particle was a beautiful diamond. The tears were coming together and forming an enormous arch that began transitioning into the brightest and most beautiful of colors. God had created a rainbow out of the Angels' sorrowful tears as a reward for their sacrifice. All sadness and distress was instantly forgotten by this beautiful gift. They were now overjoyed to have beaten the victim if it meant God's happiness for them. The rainbow burst through the Heavens, arching high over the house of worship, letting the Angels know that God was pleased with their actions.

God commanded Lucifer to rise and watched the blood drip down the Angel's body. God asked:

"Why did you come forward?"

Lucifer immediately replied:

"Because you asked."

This loyal act of devotion had never been displayed before and Lucifer would now become God's most trusted member of Heaven. Lucifer was acknowledged as the second in command among their ranks and would now be God's confidant. A superior Angel among the rest because of the self-sacrifice.

A hierarchy of power had been created which would start a dark manifestation of existence, changing it forever. The sacrifice that Lucifer had made created the three most dangerous emotions: arrogance, hatred, and jealousy.

When one is given power over others it causes one to become arrogant. This arrogance is despised by those who are now ruled over and causes them to develop a hatred for the one in control. This hatred spawns the emotion of jealousy for the elevated superiority that the wielder of power now possesses. Those that are now controlled will begin to conspire against the one in power in order to remove them from their position of authority.

This new era of emotion within Heaven brought with it dark and evil ways that no Angel thought could ever be. God was pleased with the new invention and saw it as a new form of dominance with unlimited potential.

The love that the Angels felt for God was so powerful that they now felt the need to perform vicious acts against one another and by doing so there was the possibility of receiving additional love. Angels were willing to do anything that could put them in better favor with God for they too desired to feel the power that Lucifer was given.

God's presence was now inaccessible to the common Angel. It was a gift and would only be bestowed in the most important of circumstances. Lucifer would be the messenger to the collective group of worshipers.

The other Angels were not as significant in Heaven's new hierarchy and Lucifer, as second in command, was now feared because of the power available; the power to summon the wrath of God. Lucifer reveled in this new position and felt love for the new function of power. The original equality among the Angels was no more.

This power resulted in a self-righteous arrogance. No Angel was superior to the second in command and Lucifer developed a feeling of disgust and contempt for the others. Lucifer had the ability to command the Angels and felt a desire to retaliate against the brutality they had inflicted. Lucifer spoke to God, asking for revenge against the others and it was granted.

Chapter 9

Revenge

God knew that this gift of revenge would secure loyalty and create a further divide among the other Angels. The Angels were loyal subjects of worship but had now turned into pawns. They were merely pieces of a world that God was free to manipulate and influence in order to sustain a combative hierarchy. Heaven was becoming a dramatic theatre for God's pleasure. God would toy with Lucifer and the Angels by encouraging conflict to ultimately receive more love from all of them.

This new game of power and deceit was underway and it excited God to think of how Heaven would progress now that these new events were about to unfold. Lucifer began taking revenge upon the Angels. Flying wildly throughout Heaven and singling out Angels that were seen as performing unfit worship. They were then belittled and ridiculed by Lucifer for their inability to show God how grateful they were to be in Heaven. Lucifer threatened to erase their existence and taunted the Angels, telling them that God would not notice if they ceased to exist.

This was a turbulent time in Heaven and the Angels were confused by the lack of God's presence and afraid that they would become obsolete if they didn't heed Lucifer's demands. There was a painful sorrow that all of the Angels felt and Lucifer wanted it to continue.

Lucifer decided to impress God with an event that would allow ultimate revenge on all of the Angels. God had to be appeased and the only way to do so was through sacrifice and brutality.

Lucifer asked God's permission to create this orchestrated demonstration of sacrifice and it was granted.

Chapter 10

The Sacrifice for Love

Violence is what Lucifer craved for the sacrifice and knew that blood would have to be spilled in order for God to be satisfied. Twelve Angels were needed for this event.

Lucifer began hunting for the Angels that would be part of this affair and flew throughout Heaven searching for the chosen ones. Joy was felt upon seeing the Angels cower in the dunes of Heaven as they hid from what they could only imagine would be a horrid task they must perform. The Angels that Lucifer chose for the event were the most subservient and meekest among the others. The most humble and submissive Angels would be more easily influenced to be part of the plan to impress God. From this observation, Lucifer was able to choose twelve very timid and fearful subjects for the sacrifice.

The twelve were scared of what they were chosen for but also felt important to have been summoned. The Angels were assured that God had chosen them and that they would be given an amazing gift upon completing this undertaking.

Their level of devoutness would finally be rewarded.

This filled the Angels with hope as they anticipated the unfolding of the events to come. Their minds raced with excitement as they felt the prospect of having an elevated status among the ranks of Heaven.

The other Angels, outside of the chosen twelve, heard the call of the bell to worship. They sprinted up the heavenly mountain steps and upon entering the Angels saw that the landscape had changed. God had added rows around the floor of the temple that tiered upwards. The house was now a stadium to observe events that would transpire below. The Angels were above their usual place on the floor where they had previously knelt and felt like they had moved up in the hierarchy of Heaven. God was no longer forcing them to kneel but had accepted them at a higher place, closer to the throne.

The Angels gathered in the stands with passions running high as they awaited the turn of events, peering anxiously down to the floor. They desired to know the purpose of this occasion and also felt a tinge of jealousy as to why they were not a part of the chosen group. The jealousy turned to anger and quickly escalated with the building of emotional momentum. This energy created a ripple effect among their ranks as they began to act as a collective force of passion, which was full of rage and resentment for the others. They had evolved into an angry and jealous mob of shared emotion. Easily influenced by a singular motive but not strong enough to offer an opposing reasonable argument and all fueled with hate and envy. A mob needs a leader, a separate influential voice that can be followed blindly. That leader was Lucifer. The second in command enticed the horde of eager Angels, letting them wait in excited fervor until their lust for the knowledge of the event could no longer be delayed.

God loved this added chaos and had known Lucifer would take advantage of the gift of power. The Angels believed they had moved up in Heaven's ranks now that they sat just below the throne instead of bowing on the coliseum floor and the chosen twelve felt more elite since they had been selected for this performance. Their world was developing and evolving now that power was filtering through their structure. Power cannot stand on its own, it has to be empowered by another. That empowerment came from God.

There was nothing more valuable to God than control, and the Angels had unknowingly become slaves to their master. They were servants that needed to be dominated and manipulated.

The chosen twelve Angels were ordered to wait at the bottom of the stairway.

Lucifer stood at the center of the floor, looking around the coliseum at the Angels who were salivating and roaring for the event to begin. Lucifer knelt on the floor and bowed, paused for a brief moment, and then surged upward in flight. The wings billowed with strength as the lead Angel swerved in a graceful arc, sailing around the stands where the Angels waited.

Circling the coliseum in an arrogant show of power, Lucifer whipped around with a confident assurance of command in Heaven.

This display worked the Angels into a crazed fury. They cheered and shouted as they witnessed Lucifer flying close to God's throne. They began chanting the name:

"Lucifer, Lucifer, Lucifer!"

The words rang throughout Heaven and vibrated against the walls of the coliseum. The Angels felt that they were a part of a collective. Powerless alone but together they felt strong as members of the mob.

Without notice, God let out a random shuddering clap of thunder, a command for silence.

Lucifer dropped like a stone from spiraling around the throne and landed in the middle of the floor of worship.

Delighted at the ability to control the Angels, Lucifer gave a superior commanding stare to all of them.

Heaven's bell tolled and the twelve knew their time had come. Ascending the stairway to Heaven was usually an emotionally taxing trip, full of feelings of inadequacy and despair but today seemed different. They felt privileged climbing the steps with their heads held high and were fanatical to enter the temple knowing Lucifer had hand-picked them to represent the rest of God's flock. It would be their time to be held in an esteemed position above the rest. Running up the steps the Angels were fueled by a powerful energy brought on by the expectation of reward for their faithful praise. Their time in existence had come. The Angels powered through God's house, sprinted past the pillars and stopped in the middle of the floor.

Chapter 11

Betrayal

And now Lucifer's plan came to fruition, the first betrayal was made.

Lucifer had successfully tempted the Angels by preying on their simple desire for power. The possibility of receiving a position of authority for these chosen twelve was so great that they did not think to question any ulterior motive. The offer had seemed genuine and easily earned the trust of the submissive Angels. Lucifer had effortlessly influenced the docile group of obedient and weak Angels by cementing this false sense of hope and trust. They craved acceptance from their peers and were willing to embark on any journey they thought would lead them closer to God. Lucifer had taken full advantage of their lack of confidence and knew their impressionable manner would succumb to the tools of influence. The naive Angels were the perfect match for the plan.

Lucifer spoke to the chosen Angels regarding the purpose of the event:

"To show your loyalty to God you will combat each other until each of you can no longer move and lay bleeding on the floor of this great house. Your required purpose is to endure brutality and pain, to sacrifice yourselves for the glory of God."

The twelve Angels stared in disbelief as their hopes vanished and dropped to their knees in tears as the full truth of the betrayal was revealed. They felt manipulated for their submissive nature and immediately doubted their purpose in existence. A vacuum of despair formed within each and the will to live withdrew from inside.

It began with a simple chime of God's bell. The Angels knew what they had to do and flung themselves at each other. They fought not out of hate for one another but to entertain their master and feed the mob of Angels.

The Angels bludgeoned each other with a ferocity that had never been seen before. The fighting raged as blunt arms and legs met the heads and bodies of the sacrificial Angels. Blood gushed profusely from the wounds that were inflicted and tears flowed down their faces in great streams of sorrow. The sobbing Angels created small pools on the floor that grew and flooded the battleground of Heaven. The tears mixed with the blood and formed a shallow crimson pond that started stretching towards the edge of the floor. Some of the Angels began to succumb to their wounds, collapsing in pain and exhaustion they lay motionless in the red expanding pools of blood and tears.

The spectating Angels shouted and mocked as the fighting continued. Brutality was rewarded with shouts of approval from the stands and any act of mercy was discouraged by roars of negativity.

There were no winners in this battle and it continued until each Angel was rendered immobile.

The bodies of the fallen Angels started to float in the bloodied water that had pooled in the coliseum and drifted towards the entrance of the house. One by one, their limp and beaten figures poured down its mountainous side in a grotesque spewing and thrashing, head over heels tumble from the brutal peak, marking the conclusion of the conflict. Their bodies were again motionless, lying strewn and heaped in ragged form on the ground at the base of the mountain. The blood and tears of the Angels had flowed down with them, staining the brilliant white sand. The sand reacted to the combination of blood and tears and formed a compact, dense, burgundy-brown landmass that could not be blown away like the wisping sand of Heaven. This new solid region around the base of the kingdom would be a permanent reminder of this tragic conflict.

A terribly still silence engulfed Heaven as the first battle in existence was now complete. The mob of Angels was hushed in anguished torn emotion at the conclusion of the massacre. They couldn't help feeling they had betrayed their own kind by letting them suffer.

God ordered them to leave the house of worship in a hurried thunderous dismissal. The mob raced away from the horrific scene in agonized confusion, hurling themselves down the steps only to meet the tragedy once again as they stumbled upon the fallen Angels at the bottom of the mountain. Overcome with emotion upon seeing their fallen comrades they fell to their knees and cradled the bodies of their Heavenly companions. Crying out in agony at the state of affairs in their realm.

God then commanded the twelve afflicted Angels to rise in flight, an invitation to the base of their master's throne. They were instantly healed and beat their strong wings dry from the bloodied tear filled pools until they radiated white once again. They soared back up the mountain with the renewed strength of God's grace and each felt the strength of ten Angels as they ascended back to the temple. The mob of Angels stared in perplexed bewilderment as they were left behind, watching the chosen few fly back to the scene of the battle.

All twelve knelt at the foot of God's throne, knowing they had been chosen for being the most humble and dedicated of worshipers, proving the extent of their unwavering loyalty. They were then given the gift of power from God, an elevated position as trusted Disciples.

It was an honor to be given an identity from God. The Disciples now represented a group of Angels in command of the others and were only below Lucifer in Heaven's hierarchy. They would act as God's counsel, not as high ranking as Lucifer but a group that would now control the other Angels. The Disciples saw themselves as a collective power. The combined power of twelve was a forceful unit that could rival and challenge the authority of Lucifer.

The Disciple's feelings of irrelevance was eliminated when God bestowed the valued gift of power to them. Their convictions had been restored and it was believed that God did this out of love.

Lucifer observed this turn of events and could not help the overwhelming feeling of resentment toward the newly chosen group. Lucifer felt threatened by the hierarchal change and for the first time, began to think a bit differently about the true purpose God had for the members of existence.

Chapter 12

Order is Restored

God's use of power, manipulation, and control among the Angels was remarkable. Only God knew what had truly been accomplished by these planned events.

God had known that this would bring about questions among the members of existence. It was all part of a plan to strengthen the hold on the Angels that would ultimately result in more worship. God's arrogance required the creation of situations that would bring about additional measures of praise from the Angels.

God had used Lucifer's desire for vengeance as the catalyst to invoke this ferocious act. The others had then banned together in a bloodthirsty mob, tantalized with the hope of achieving greater status, which resulted in a desire to witness the destruction of their fellow Angels. The Disciples, through a necessary sacrifice, had laid the foundation of this change to existence and had been a required piece to execute the plan. All had played their part in the manipulative game that God had spun into effect.

The orchestration of these horrific events had instilled

uncertainty among the Angels regarding their place and purpose in Heaven.

There was disarray in Heaven since the battle and order had to be restored. Confidence had to be given back to the Angels so they would again feel purpose and a reason to exist. God would right the balance of Heaven now that the well-planned events had taken shape, giving way to the next plot.

God addressed Heaven:

"I love you all and I always have. You are all forgiven for what you have done. There will be no more sacrifices in Heaven and you will never combat each other again. No longer shall we soak the Heavens with your blood and instead we will create another existence. You will help me design a world that will sacrifice itself for our greatness and we will build it together in the image of Heaven. I am the God of existence, but you, you now have the ability to take my power and will use it to create, destroy, and rule."

And with that, the Angels once again became aware of their purpose. God's coordinated battle had debased them to nothing and had broken their spirits. This caused them to question their commitment.

The revelation of God's new plan solidified their loyalty and resulted in even greater love and devotion for their leader.

These actions created the most devoted of subjects for they now believed they did not have the intellect to comprehend the necessary actions of their master.

A new inspiration of undying loyalty and an unquestioning following had been built. God had created this and would now build a new world for the Angels to control.

Heaven gathered as a collective; Lucifer, the new Disciples, and the rest of the Angels. All together and equally awestruck by the majesty of their God.

God spoke:

"Show me your worth by creating a world worthy of our

supremacy."

Heaven began to tremble with thunder.

God internally thought:

"I am God and no one will ever question me! Let it begin."

God sent an explosion of white-hot beaming light from the throne that propelled a massive shockwave through Heaven, forcing the Angels to kneel and look away. When the wave had passed they stood and looked behind them. Shining above was a massive ball of fire so brilliant that you could not look at it. It flamed and boiled as its surface erupted with light and heat. It was so massive and great that it took the breath away from the Angels in one shared gasp. This mighty sphere, burning in flame and light, was the Sun of God, built in God's image.

The Sun's brightness was a force to be worshiped and all who looked upon it would have to bow and shield themselves from its raw power. The power of God.

The Sun would provide life to the new world and the entities that the Angels would choose to create would have to worship its greatness. Just like worshiping God, no one could get too close to the Sun and no one could look directly at it. This would be the origin of the new world. The rays of the Sun enabled the Angels, giving them the power of God, the power to create.

Chapter 13

Creation Part 1

The Angels would now worship God by creating a new world in the image of Heaven. None of the Angels were sure how to proceed. They had never created before, only worshiped. Only one Angel knew how to think beyond the collective to start creation, Lucifer.

Lucifer knew this world had to be special and different from what they knew in Heaven. God only appreciated original thought and Lucifer felt the need to prove the status given by God as second in command.

Lucifer asked God for a small piece of the great Sun and God granted the request. Lucifer then took Heaven's sand and threw it at the acquired portion of the Sun. The sand melted around it, hardening into a spherical mass of rock. The piece of Sun became the core of the new planet. God was a literal part of the world and God's greatness came from above and below. All life would be forced to worship.

God saw the solid world and was pleased. Lucifer then spun the world in a constant motion so that every face of the planet would have to wait in darkness until the Sun reappeared again to bask the planet in warmth. A full rotation would be called a day, a day of worshiping the Sun. This new piece of existence would also gradually rotate around the Sun in orbit. Once a full orbit was complete it would represent a year of worshipping Sun. Not only had Lucifer created a new world, but also the measurement of time. Time was a function of the planet revolving around the Sun of God.

Lucifer had again proven to be the perfect choice for God's second in command. God could not have been more pleased with this new world and just like Heaven, everything revolved around God.

While Lucifer was preoccupied with creating the new world, the Disciples had taken the opportunity to gain favor in Heaven with the other Angels. They had strength in numbers and began a campaign against Lucifer's commanding authority. Preaching to the other Angels to join them in the task of creating a world that God would love. The Disciples promised the Angels that the opportunity of gaining power in Heaven awaited if they joined forces. The mob of Angels needed guidance and decided quickly and without question that the Disciples would be their trusted leaders.

This was the start of a divide between Lucifer and the rest of Heaven. The Disciples were now ruling over the other Angels and had captured power while Lucifer had started the creation of the new world.

The Disciples knew God loved violence and saw the world as a battlefield, a proving ground to gain power. It would be a competition between the Angels and Lucifer to win God's love.

Lucifer's approach was to create beauty and originality in order to show God something magnificent and extraordinary. Lucifer had transformed since the days of manipulating the Angels and no longer craved power as much since given

God's task of creation. To Lucifer, creation was the greatest gift that God could have ever presented and this diminished the previous desire for power. Creation was the beauty of existence and was the closest thing to God. It was all Lucifer really craved.

God saw the evolvement of Heaven and was overjoyed. God again had a new scheme to occupy the reign of existence. Lucifer and the Disciples would continue to battle and plot against each other. A perfect atmosphere was being created that would form a constant struggle of violent and dramatic affairs, all having the result of additional praise and love.

Giving Lucifer and the Disciples power gave them hope that they were in God's grace but unbeknownst to them, it was merely a game of arrogant manipulation that God created in order to ensure continued love and worship.

And so the competition started with the Disciples who reacted with their own form of creativity for this new world. All life would require another form of Heaven to grow and survive. It would be a part of every aspect of life and everything would crave it. This would be a part of the Angels and it was their tears. This pure form of water would come from them and cover the world that Lucifer had made. The Disciples began to torment their subjects in order to extract the tears that were necessary to immerse the new world. They intimidated and bullied the Angels, making them feel inadequate regarding their loyalty to the new mission. The harassment continued until each Angel wept uncontrollably at the cruelty brought on by the Disciples. The tears rained down to Lucifer's sphere and covered the globe in water, making the solid mass no longer visible. Water now covered every inch of the surface. It had been drowned by the vindictiveness of the Disciples. They had taken the glory from Lucifer by changing the world, an action done out of jealousy.

Lucifer, enraged by the changes to the world, grasped the

hardened land from beneath God's kingdom. The land that had been stained by the blood spilled during the brutal conflict that spawned the creation of the Disciples. Lucifer threw massive pieces at the planet and the scattered particles sank to the bottom of the vast bodies of water. The land accumulated until it spilled over the water's surface, creating enormous grounds spanning the globe. The bloodied-brown land from Heaven was now the land of the new world.

When the land of Heaven settled, God gave the world a name, Earth. This Earth would have the ability to create on its own and it would grow life from the land of Heaven that was now the soil of Earth. The tears of the Angels would be the fuel of life that everything would require. The Sun, Earth, and water would be the foundation of life and all beings would be connected in this newly shared existence.

Chapter 14

Creation Part 2

The Earth had a foundation that was ready to flourish with new life. Lucifer's vision was to create beauty. God-pleasing magnificent splendor that would bring awe to all who gazed upon it. The first idea for life that would thrive in this new environment would originate in the ground and worship the Sun, always growing closer to it. This would be flora, the first life on Earth. Lucifer began blanketing the grounds with luscious plants and greenery. It was a majesty of opulent and majestic colors with a variety of different identities and types. They were rich, warm, and grew to perfection from the rays of the Sun. Their life brought luscious scents and crisp aromas of fragrance that were abundant and pure. The plants covered the globe with varying shades of greens, purples, reds, deep blues, and pinks. Flora grew towards the sky and covered every piece of Earth. It was the most untouched and expansive beauty that had ever been seen.

The Angels witnessed this beauty and had to find a way to limit the continuous growth. Lucifer could not have all matter of creativity and never be challenged. The Disciples met with the Angels to counter Lucifer.

How could they stop this beautiful creativity? They met as the mob with the Disciples acting as a council that presided over the yelling and bickering among the Angels. Halting the arguments, the Disciples decided to take a part of Heaven's massive cloud formation that swirled about their world in an attempt to block out the energy that the Sun supplied to the life of flora. Beating their wings in unison the Angels created a gust of powerful wind that raged and blew the clouds from Heaven to Earth. The thick clouds billowed and blocked out the Sun, the lifeblood of the luscious plants that Lucifer had created.

The clouds also swept over the bodies of water and began circulating the Earth, growing with the tears of the Angels they rained down and flooded the land. What had been meant as a form of retaliation now became a reward. The Angels had unintentionally created an atmosphere that would distribute the Angel tears and fuel the plants of the world. The water would help them grow, prosper, and become even more beautiful.

Lucifer was victorious and the Angels' plan had backfired.

The Angels were enraged by this and had to retaliate. They decided to change the position of the Earth relative to the Sun. They went to God's mountain and began to extract massive stones from its base and hurled these rocks at the Earth in an onslaught of meteors. The boulders sped to Earth in tremendous trails of fire, streaking across the sky and then exploding on the globe. This created gigantic craters all across the Earth's surface and the explosions caused the ground to burst into immense clouds of dust that blocked out the Sun. The bombardment of the Earth continued until the combined power of the continuous assault tilted the Earth on an axis, creating the seasons. There would now be times of intense cold and heat in certain parts of the Earth as it traveled around the Sun causing the stifling of flora's rapid growth. The Angels had limited Lucifer's creations from constantly expanding and had defeated part of Lucifer's vision.

The massive stones from Heaven had also created something else by mistake. The rocks that were thrown to Earth had detonated with such force that pieces of them broke away and traveled back out of Earth's atmosphere. The Angels, in their fitful combative rage, had created the stars of what was now turning into a galaxy. Thrilled with these new additions the Angels took more pieces of God's mountain and threw them into the space around the Earth. These pieces became new planets that glistened brightly in the distance from the surface of Earth.

The strife between the Angels and Lucifer was the origin of the Solar System. Angels cared only about defeating Lucifer and destroying the beauty that Lucifer had created in order to please God. Lucifer, however, wanted the beauty of original creation to impress God. The battle for approval continued and God reflected positively on the developments.

The Earth, its inhabitants, and the surrounding solar system had become a game and now there was a circle of life forming that would yield even greater turmoil. It was a controlled battle of creation that reflected the real conflict that was going on in Heaven. The galaxy, Earth, and the lives on it were the weapons in this cosmic war of dominance and power. It was all merely a game of control for God's ever-growing arrogance.

Lucifer stood apart from this rivalry and took actual joy in creating with no ulterior motive of gaining power. Original creation could only bring a closer relationship to God. Lucifer's desire for power had changed and Lucifer believed God's love could be received through continued creation and not by combatting the Angels.

Chapter 15

The State of the Earth

The pure clean atmosphere of Earth produced a cooling soft air that flowed peacefully and caressed the water, plants, and land of the world. There were no storms, just an effortless harmony of elements working together with nothing threatening the other. It was a bountiful beauty of an untainted environment.

The land of Earth was the deep red-brown color of the blood-soaked Heavens. Its richness provided the nutrients of life for the plants that blossomed within it. The land was warm, thick, and oily. It almost dripped with the sustenance of soft richness. The soil was the start of all life and carried the pureness of the blood of the Angels. It had their original innocence of love as its integrity. This love from the soil could be seen within every piece of plant life on Earth. The ground had only known growth and creation and there was nothing that spoiled the purity of nature. The plants continued to evolve by yielding brighter colors with richer textures and quickly sprang to life within the sweet soil of an unrestricted open environment. The rich existence on Earth was developing rapidly and at a quicker pace than Heaven had expected.

The water from the tears of the Angels were the vast oceans that covered the planet. Water was the lifeblood of every living being. It came from the Heavens and rained on all matter of life, quenching the plants need for moisture. It pooled in great seas and lakes across the Earth and lapped the soft soils of land. Its moisture was soft and loving and cooled the Earth from the scorch of the bright Sun.

Life on Earth had no knowledge of Heaven. There was peace among the elements that existed on Earth. The Heavens had created a harmonious place outside of their realm, which was thought to not be possible. Through their battles amongst each other there now existed a place without the arrogance and jealous nature of Heaven. Earth stood alone, a symbol of what Heaven could be, a peaceful existence. On Earth, there was no desire for the trappings of what the Angels thought was necessary in Heaven. There wasn't a lust for power or a competitive desire to outdo each other in order to gain a more favorable hierarchical position. The Earth only lived and provided what was needed without the desire to conquer in this virtuous natural oasis. A preserve of harmony that would continue to exist without flaw, this was life on Earth.

The pure natural world continued to evolve and develop in ways that were unexpected. Plants developed the ability to change and to keep growing in different ways; taller, bigger, yielding fruits and seeds to expand their coexistence on Earth. Their internal desires were not to be better than one another but to progress with a common goal of existing in peace. They used the water and nutrients of the Earth to live in a flawless collective of undisturbed beauty that would flourish for eternity. Their purpose was to live a life within the natural existence of harmony.

Chapter 16

The Soul

The creation of life created the force of wanting to live. The plants of the Earth were conscious beings that believed in helping their kind develop, improve, and flourish. They had an overall sense of wanting to help one another for the greater good of the collective that they were all a part of. The flora of Earth existed in a unified way of life.

The plants were able to communicate in a silent language even though they were segregated by vast areas of land and were of a different species. It was a language of senses, emotion, and of a common touch. Their communication flowed with the swaying of the winds and circulation of the atmosphere. The wind carried their collective language across the globe, touching each plant on the Earth. It was an invisible sense that they all possessed. Where every plant had the ability to reach out to the next through this natural life connection.

There was also was another part, a part unbeknownst to Heaven. An unseen aura that each plant was bestowed once created. This was a soul.

The soul was the eternal life that mirrored the Angels. The plants grew from the blood and tears of the Angels and were fueled by the Sun of God. These elements that gave them life were all part of Heaven. To be created by Heaven meant that the new creations of Earth were also a part of it and had the gift of eternal life. They were true members of Heaven and could exist forever on Earth.

This form of creation was an unforeseen accident of life. The thought of adding something new and different to existence seemed impure to God and the Angels. There was a system of hierarchy and power in Heaven.

How could something live forever outside of it? This started confusion and anger among the Angels. If Lucifer could create everlasting life on Earth how was that different from God? God felt challenged and would not allow souls to exist for eternity outside of Heaven. Lucifer and the Angels had done well with their creation of the new world but God's power could not be seen as replicable. If God was to stay in power God had to change life on Earth by ending it.

Chapter 17

Death

God created death, an end to all life. Life would now deteriorate with the passage of time, which meant that eventually all life would come to an end on Earth. God did not create these beings and did not want peace and eternal life on Earth. There had to be control over this new world and Lucifer's power to create. Death would make life finite and give God the pleasure of ending the creations that Lucifer had made.

The invention of death was immediately recognized to life and caused flora to fear it. They feared the end of their conscious lives for they were not ready to die and didn't know if they had ever lived life to the fullest.

True control is the denial of knowledge, and God would let life be tortured with the fear of the unknown, life after death. This would be life's eternal struggle, the fight to live for fear of death.

The true potential of life can only be achieved by knowing that there is eternal life, without that awareness, life cannot be truly experienced.

Lucifer had enjoyed creation and had evolved out of the lust of power that plagued Heaven. The living world, in Lucifer's mind, was meant to just live and exist in harmony. Life was not meant to be harmed or to be judged. Life on Earth was meant to live with a shared vision of unity among its inhabitants.

God was pleased with the application of death but furious that Lucifer's creative ability had undermined the structure of Heaven. Order had to be restored yet again and God rang Heaven's bell, the call to worship.

God addressed Lucifer:

"I am the ruler of existence, creator of all life. The only reason your creations on Earth exist is because I allow it. It is not your creativity that has made life, it is mine. I made you and you have no ability to create unless I grant it. You only exist because of me and do not forget that. I alone can end all matter of life whenever I choose."

God's voice echoed with great blasts of thunder. Lightning cracked around the Angels, striking the floor of God's coliseum thousands of times, causing it to glow with heat below the huddled kneeling forms of the Angels.

"You created life and I destroyed it by creating death. All matter of life will writhe on Earth with fear of the afterlife. They do not deserve our Heaven and will die never knowing if they truly lived. The fear of the unknown will always hold back the true potential of life. Upon their death, I will keep the souls as my own and they will swirl in the clouds of Heaven for eternity in a constant state of confusion and sorrowful disarray with no purpose. This is the fate of the souls you created."

And so it was. An endless confusion was the fate for the souls of Earth. They would swirl in Heaven in an endless churning vortex above God's throne and would never know Heaven nor have the joy while alive to be aware that they could pass on to another state of existence. A fate derived by

God out of selfish desire and lust for control over others.

The balance had been restored in Heaven and opportunity had now presented itself. The love Lucifer felt for creation was seen as a weakness to the Disciples.

How could Lucifer have shown affection for the creation of life? Love was only meant for God and nothing else. The Disciples' observation of Lucifer's weakness fueled their desire to elevate themselves within the ranks of Heaven.

Lucifer, wanting to please God, was motivated to create again. However, there was no longer a desire to achieve this by inventing a form of sacrifice that involved pain and suffering. Lucifer would bring God other forms of life. These new creations would be more original and innovative than anything in existence. They would be created out of the spirit of what Earth represented, a balanced harmony built around a unified life. Lucifer's hope was that if God could see the Earth existing in a state of equality then it could possibly change the way God ruled the Heavens.

With the longing for change, Lucifer again created.

Chapter 18

Creation Part 3

Fauna commenced into the splendor of Earth's expansive bodies of water, the oceans. The vast depths of the sea would be the start of all new forms of life.

Lucifer started by creating a foundation of intricate coral ecosystems that spread throughout the oceans. Life centered around these elaborate structures and other creatures spawned from them and also relied on them to survive. The sea was a rich, bountiful, and fascinating place with so many diverse types of life. From the minutest organisms that were barely visible, to the titanic beasts that dwarfed the other ocean dwellers. The individuality of the countless ocean inhabitants echoed the originality of the plants and the beauty of the ocean life was immeasurable.

The beautiful land and expansive sky were next to be blessed by creativity. The creatures spanned the globe from the frigid poles, scorching deserts, to the lush forests. They were all different, unique, and had an elegant beauty that showed the brilliance of Lucifer's ability to create. The many lives of fauna were intelligent and resourceful beings that mastered their surroundings. From the massive to the small, they roamed the lands and soared the skies in vast numbers.

The great expanse of nature was their home and the animals became one with what they were given.

Their lives moved and flowed in a harmonic array of living that was all connected in a web of life that surged throughout all of them. It gave them an understanding of each other, an invisible force of nature that bound and linked everything. The animals were a part of the environment and it shaped a universal form of communication that all Earthly species could understand. There was a conscious feeling that all life was in touch with the other. The plants and animals felt it through the wind, rain, and soil. The Earth spoke to them through its constantly changing ecosystem and they could feel the coldness of the poles, the heat of the desserts, the movement and depth of the seas. Each life living separately but part of the whole. It was a natural connection of existence. It was a life to live and nothing more.

There was pure peace between flora and fauna. It was an appreciation for each other and their bountiful home. They did not desire more and were never harmed by another. Water was the only longing they had, the only form of sustenance necessary to keep on living. It was the framework of everything and all matter relied on it. The tears of the Angels that had fallen from unspeakable cruelty now supplied Earth with the only energy necessary to live.

It was Lucifer's subconscious that created this harmonious environment. What Lucifer truly desired in Heaven was echoed with the creation of Earth. Peace and equality among all life.

Lucifer knew that God would not be satisfied with peace. God wanted violence, chaos, and drama for this new world. Life on Earth was a game meant for God's entertainment, a game of sacrifice.

Lucifer loved God above all and ultimately desired nothing more than to please the great ruler of existence. The lives of Earth would have to be sacrificed in order to make God content. With a heavy guilty conscience, Lucifer decided to add a new element of life to appease the Heaven's. This would be the requirement to kill in order to survive.

Chapter 19

Killer Instinct

Lucifer created an instinct that would require each life to take more than water to survive. A killer instinct was given to life, built into its foundation. This would require the killing and consumption of another life in order to keep living.

Lucifer's love for God could not be forgotten and was so great that it made the terrible necessary, the horrific act of killing.

The creation of the killer instinct threw Lucifer into turmoil. The Angel's uncertainty originated from not being able to understand why it would please God to see these beautiful, intelligent, and peaceful creatures kill one another. Their beauty had been created for God.

Why couldn't God be pleased with another part of existence? Why couldn't the lives of Earth have knowledge of Heaven and exist in harmony without killing? These questions went unanswered. The Almighty had to be pleased and Lucifer had no choice but to do so.

Chapter 20

God's Grace is Returned

God summoned Lucifer to the throne.

"You have created a value to life that will give these forms a purpose. They will kill one another for the glory of Heaven."

And now God gave the first compliment.

"You have done well Lucifer."

It was the only personal praise God had ever bestowed upon an Angel.

The knowledge of God's compliment to Lucifer spread quickly through the ranks of the Disciples and then on to their gang of Angels. Both groups were jealous of the event and disappointed in their own inability of original thought that seemed to flourish within Lucifer. They were only able to act defensively with the goal of tarnishing the gift of ingenuity in order to diminish God's grace. The mob lacked any real form of imagination and began to place blame upon each other through their shared frustrations.

The compliment given to Lucifer was a major blow to

their constant campaign against the chosen Angel. The Angels schemed amongst each other, all with the goal of overtaking Lucifer's prized position among the ranks of Heaven.

The integrity of Heaven had transformed into a world that lusted for power and it was fueled on jealousy and hate.

God knew of the Disciples hatred for Lucifer and their now constant plotting, as well as Lucifer's guilt for loving the creations of Earth. God loved this form of existence for it had become a game of brutality and death. Lucifer had surprised God with the idea of killing and God was delighted that it added a new function to Earth. Killing caused life to end and upon death, there was now control of every soul, both animal, and plant. God's dominance and control over existence reigned supreme.

Chapter 21

The Age of the Kill

Heaven was fascinated by the killing of life and was ready to observe how it would transpire. It began while Heaven watched with lusting anticipation for their new theatre.

There was a switch and the lives of Earth immediately reacted to it. Their purpose was now to take life in order to live. The desire was instilled with the killer instinct and it was not a choice, it was now a function of life.

Killing was a brutal and painful occurrence that created dreadful and sorrowful emotions for the lives of Earth. The taker of life felt internal pain and torment at the thought of killing another and the life being killed was petrified, fearing the unknown after death for they did not know what awaited after Earth.

Would they turn into nothing? Would they be reunited with the other forms of life that had been killed?

However, it did not become a game of power to the lives of Earth as Heaven had hoped. They did not use killing as a way to gain control nor did they take pleasure in taking life.

The peaceful harmonious connection that Lucifer created among Earth's inhabitants gave them all a mutual understanding of what was necessary to live for they had evolved a sense of life integrity. They were aware of their new instinct and decided as one that only the oldest lives would be killed for the survival of the others. Life connected through the elements of Earth and through those elements they were united and able to communicate, to sense the lives of the others.

The eldest members of flora and fauna sacrificed themselves to the other animals in order for them to survive within the oceans and on land. They connected to the other creatures, telling them where to find them so that killing was only done when necessary. It was nature's way of responding to the killer instinct with a sacrifice of itself in order for others to survive.

Heaven had wanted a power struggle of pain, violence, and an endless circle of brutality. Life had developed outside of Heaven's control and had countered their given instinct with continued loyalty to the fabric of their serene existence. Their way of life was only meant to help one another.

The age of the kill had failed and Earth had unknowingly outwitted Heaven. On Earth, there was no desire for power, only peace and coexistence. Lucifer's design of life caused it to overcome the killer instinct and had instead made it into a tool of self-sacrifice to help another life. Earth had risen above the violent nature that killing was meant to stand for. The power to take another life was not for personal gain but only to help another life in need.

Killing was meant to be Lucifer's gift to God. A form of redemption due to the disappointment with the other creations. Lucifer's love for Earth had overridden the original love for God and this was a betrayal.

All had failed, the Earth, the new lives on it, and the invention of killing. God wanted to rule Earth in the same manner as Heaven, to dominate it. Life on Earth believed in nothing and lived without fear of God. It was a disgrace and it would not continue to exist in this manner.

Chapter 22

The Throne of God

Lucifer was now without a purpose in Heaven and was to blame for all of Earth's shortcomings. The Angel could no longer hold the position as God's second in command and was seen as a blasphemous disappointment to their realm.

Heaven stirred with lightning. It burst and cracked on the steps to God's house as the Angels heeded the tolling of the bell, climbing with the thunder crackling and erupting above. It called to them, fed their thought with a lust for what was to come. The Disciples and their flock of Angels ascended the steps with an energy that they had not felt before. This would be their time and they knew that a change to Heaven's hierarchy was an opportunity.

Each Angel mocked and jeered Lucifer as they passed the now rejected Angel on the staircase to God's house. The Angels proclaimed the worthlessness of the Earth as they ascended together and were overwrought with anticipation at the prospect of gaining power due to the failed creations. Lucifer's head hung low with wings dragging in dread for what was to come. The punishment of God, feared above all else.

Lucifer climbed the steps with eyes closed, tears began to lightly stream down the face of the once revered being. It was a slow, fearful, and dejected ascent to the top. The love for creation had been seen as absolute failure.

The Angels waited at the top of the stairway for Lucifer. Thunder boomed and stormed with ferocity as God tantalized the mob, feeding their desire for power. The Angels celebrated in unthinkable cruelty as they awaited the arrival of their once feared leader.

Upon mounting thc last step Lucifer was met with a blow to the face by the first Disciple. Reeling from the force, Lucifer fell backward only to be thrown into the arms of another Angel. What then began was a gauntlet of continuous thrashing and pummeling by the others. Lucifer was being passed from Angel to Angel, circulated through their crowd in what was the first orchestrated assault on another member of Heaven outside of God's command.

The Angels gratified themselves with this attack. Too long had they waited for the day when Lucifer would no longer be held in such high regard. Their day of reckoning had come.

They tormented Lucifer with vicious acts of savagery while God thundered from above with approval for the barbarity. The light of God beamed and radiated throughout Heaven, it represented satisfaction for the cruelty being performed. Lucifer was soaked in matted blood and could barely move as the Angels continuously flew to stunning heights, stalled in mid-air, and then dropped down at blistering speeds. Lucifer's frame was continuously struck by these sickening devastating crashes of momentum.

Lucifer could no longer move and was carried into the coliseum by the hands of the Angels. Hoisted above their heads in outstretched arms, a trophy for God. A trail of blood and tears followed the throng as Lucifer wept and drifted deeper into despair. The Angels roared with victory and tossed their former comrade onto the floor at the foot of the throne.

The thunder and lightning suddenly stopped, only silence remained. The Angels flew to the upper portions of the house and stood in silence in the rows of the coliseum, all looking below at the crumpled bloodied heap on the floor of the kingdom.

Tears streamed down Lucifer's face and blood pooled all around the mirrored floor, silhouetting the Angel's form. The silence continued in an overbearing stillness that God purposefully drew out so that all would know the penalty of failure. The Angels stared down at Lucifer, delighted in the disgraced appearance.

Lucifer had been untouchable as the chosen Angel. Appointed by God as a superior entity in Heaven and now debased to the lowliest being in existence. Lucifer's attempt to please God had failed and God was making it known that this would result in severe punishment.

God commanded Lucifer to fly to the top of the throne, a privilege that no Angel had ever experienced. Lucifer sprang up from the ground with a swift beat from the tattered bloodied wings and flew straight up.

The Angels looked on, filled with shock and awe at this turn of events.

How could this be, a summoning to the throne? The mighty throne that no Angel was worthy of sharing? Where God directed all of existence?

The form of Lucifer soared to the throne and God beamed a brilliant bright shining light onto the shape of the Angel. The light caused the Angel's wings to glow and melted away the blood, healing the wounds. The light replenished the force of life within Lucifer who now seemed to be guided in a powerful flight. Silence blanketed Heaven as all were focused on this resurrection. A return to God's grace.

Lucifer arrived at the throne and hovered elegantly above

it before landing. It was a round-mirrored platform of perfection that shimmered and moved as if the surface was made of water. And there was God, a beaming sphere of electric vivacious light that glared in brilliance, radiating and reflecting from the throne. God shone so brightly that Lucifer doubled over with pain from the blinding powerful blaze. The light consumed Lucifer's thoughts and physical being. It was a force that hummed and vibrated with pure white energy. The light of God shone through Lucifer and forced a kneeling position, the natural form of worship caused by the intensity. Lucifer was now on one knee as God spoke:

"You!"

God roared as a burst of light exploded out like a shock wave, rippling the glassy water like surface of the throne. It traveled as a transparent surge, flashing through Heaven, knocking Lucifer flat. The ring of light burst and ran through God's house, blasting all the Angels back against the inner walls of the coliseum. The Angels were stunned by the force of God's anger and were now breathless as they awaited the outcome of this event.

"Your sacrifice has helped build the foundation of Heaven. Without your actions and ability, we would not have our way of existence. I gave you the great power of creation, my power, and with it you were able to make the Earth and give it life that we have never seen."

The unexpected was sinking in, shock to the Disciples and Angels. They couldn't believe what was happening.

Lucifer's fear of being punished was evaporating and had been replaced with a feeling of unwavering loyalty. The Angel was being openly loved and showered with compliments. The sensation of being blessed with praise was the most beautiful and magnificent feeling in existence.

Lucifer realized that God did not intend to deal out punishment for the creation of Earth. It had been built as a tribute out of the love that Lucifer felt. God worked in mysterious ways and Lucifer knew that these actions must be for a greater purpose. This meeting between the two of them was the ultimate gift an Angel could receive.

The bright shining light of God did not hurt anymore and instead it strengthened Lucifer. They were on the same level as creators. No one could understand except for the two of them.

Chapter 23

Fall from Grace

God continued:

"After everything you have done, I no longer love you. You are not worthy to exist among us and have disgraced all of Heaven. I bestowed upon you the greatest gift, a taste of my power. You then created an Earth that defied our meaning. You will not be missed in Heaven and we will remember you and your Earth as symbols of failure and insignificance. We will recreate the Earth and you will be forced to watch our manipulation of it. You will be sent to a new domain, a pathetic world of disappointment to writhe for the rest of eternity. All the souls of life that you created will also be sent to this realm to carry out their existence knowing they are too inferior to be part of Heaven."

The foundation of Heaven was now trembling and shaking with God's rage. There was a steady vibration growing into a catastrophic climax that no one could predict.

"Lucifer, you are damned to Hell and will never to return to Heaven."

Two massive heat searing bolts of lightning erupted and sliced downward from the sky above God's throne. Sliding like liquid white steel from above, they struck the top of the cresting bend of Lucifer's wings, igniting them on fire.

Both bolts struck with the overpowering strength of God, forcing Lucifer to bend down on both knees. Lucifer's frame erupted into an inferno as thunder clapped and lightning flashed overhead. The intensity of the fire tossed Lucifer to the floor of the throne. The Angel rolled and thrashed to the edge of it and then fell. It was a fall from grace.

Lucifer saw the throne move away in slow motion, falling backward with a shocked look of sorrow and pain at the unexpected loss of everything. The fall from upon high was a blaze, a burning ball that quickly gathered speed in its decent. Every Angel was rigid and watching in ever-building excitement as Lucifer came closer to the base of the coliseum. The fire streaked in two parallel flames as the now singed wingless Lucifer plummeted to the floor of the palace. As Lucifer was just about to hit the floor it opened into a black vacuum, which was Hell. The Angel, who was once the hand of God, had vanished and the flame went out. God spoke to the remaining Angels:

"I will now remake the Earth and its meaningless inhabitants into an existence that is worthy of Heaven. Any challengers to the superiority of my Heaven will suffer the same fate as Lucifer, eternal damnation to Hell."

"My faithful Angels, you will never walk the steps to my kingdom again. You will fly to meet me in my house and we will work together to decide the fate of Earth. We will transform the Earth and ensure that all life will fear and worship us. Let us now create!"

The Angels exploded from their observatory positions and rose to God's throne in a massive unified flight. They shrieked in excitement at the dawn of this new age. The Angels circled God's throne, praising the decision to rid Lucifer from Heaven and for the gift to rule the lives of

Earth. The fate of the Earth had been decided.

Chapter 24

Hell

Lucifer lay in a noiseless void of pure darkness and saw nothing but an endless black expanse, this was Hell. Emptiness with absolutely no life. Lucifer's thoughts drifted in and out to the life known in Heaven and what it had been. The vision of falling backward off of God's throne while on fire played over and over again.

A searing pain suddenly jolted the outcast, the wings, they were gone! The strength and power they represented had been taken away. The memory of floating above God's palace and ruling over the other Angels seemed so surreal. No Angel had been allowed such freedom in Heaven and God had bestowed power to Lucifer alone. Now there was nothing. Lucifer was no longer a member of existence but now an exile. Banished out of Heaven as a meaningless, worthless being.

Lucifer sobbed as the feeling of insignificance saturated the fibers of the once great Angel's life. There seemed to be no reason to exist. With the absence of Heaven and without

God's love it seemed pointless. Lucifer was fit for nothing and would never be a part of anything again. God's love was gone.

Hell was a complete loveless place of despair for one to suffer knowing they could be erased and forgotten. There was no hope, only the terrifying anxiety of realizing that you were unaccepted in the world you loved and thought you belonged to.

Hell was a new form of existence but it had nothing. There was no structure, no worship, no power, and no control. None of these things could exist here in the dark Godless void.

Lucifer gradually began to realize that even though it was a tragedy to be cast out of Heaven, Hell was absent of rule.

Was this a blessing in disguise? Lucifer was the ruler of Hell and there was no God here. Worship was not required and there was no need to be constantly fearful of God's wrath.

Lucifer began to comprehend that Hell, bleak as it seemed, meant freedom. With the instant awareness of knowing God was not part of Hell Lucifer felt immediate happiness. This was a new beginning and the future of existence had changed.

The rejoicing came with many questions. Lucifer had been devoted entirely to God and had sacrificed everything to be in God's grace. God had then received a new beautiful world, which had only been created out of tribute. When that was not enough the lives of Earth were surrendered to Heaven by the invention of the killer instinct as a form of destruction for God's gratification. Recanting the formation of these life-changing events reminded Lucifer that these actions had also created a feeling within, doubt. The doubt had promptly been cast aside since it was not what God would have wanted.

Why did the innocent creatures of Earth need to die and be killed? It had been done to please God but was it actually necessary? Hell was a place without God and there would be no struggle for power in this new realm. It was a place of pure independence. A place of free will without control.

Hell would be Lucifer's new creation. There would be no fear or worship and it would be absent of the lust for power that brought along such malicious actions in Heaven. It would be Earth. The true harmonious Earth the way it was meant to be, free of death and killing. It would be a natural way of living in a state of equality. This could only exist without power and the pursuit of it.

Lucifer, still possessing the ability to create from God, was overwhelmed with the realization of the possibilities of creation and transformed the void of Hell straightaway into an image of Earth. Hell was now the true vision of Earth. A parallel existence of its environment where Lucifer could now exist independently. Finally freed from the prison of Heaven.

Chapter 25

The Souls are Expelled

Lucifer was gone, banished as a worthless former member of their great society. The Angels felt unprecedented joy and they knew everything was going to change.

God spoke to the subjects of Heaven:

"Together we will do as we see fit with Earth. We will create or destroy as we choose. Nothing outside of Heaven is worthy of our greatness and we will never include the meaningless souls that Lucifer created. The souls of flora and fauna that stir in our midst are gone."

The swirling cloud of souls in Heaven evaporated as God sent them to Lucifer's Hell.

Chapter 26

Life in Hell

All the deceased souls of creation had now transferred to Hell to be reborn into a new life. Flora erupted in a rejuvenated instantaneous explosion of life. The animals of the air, land, and sea returned to their natural habitats as the life they once had was fully restored to the splendor known on Earth, now in Hell.

The air in Hell thickened sweetly with the arrival of the new inhabitants and a new world had been born. The drifting meaningless state of confusion for the lost souls abruptly ended the moment they arrived. The souls were instantly aware of their new surroundings and conscious once again.

These were the first members of Hell. These souls had been judged as unworthy members of Heaven and tortured in purgatory. They had writhed in the clouds of Heaven without purpose or knowledge of who they were. It had been an endless despairing journey of infinite perplexity. A fitting punishment that God decided was worthy of Lucifer's mistakes. Since Lucifer had created all life that meant that they were all only worthy of being banished to Hell with their creator.

Hell was a place to live in peace with love for all other life. Lucifer had renewed the lives of Earth. The souls now had the existence intended for them and were supplied with the knowledge that life was eternal. Fear of death had vanished and the killing instinct was erased in the new home of Hell.

Hell was joy, peace, and harmony. The animals walked side by side and pranced in the beauty of Hell, which was a reflection of Earth. The air was thick and fragrant and the soil, oily and rich. They needed nothing and had nothing but love for each other. The only desire was to explore the vastness of their world and to gather together in a shared unity of eternal life with other beings. A pure place where they would live only to live.

Lucifer addressed the first members of Hell, not on a throne, but on the same level as they were. There wasn't a commanding tone or the expectation to be worshiped. The goal was to welcome and connect with the beings while enlightening them about their new place in this realm of existence.

"Welcome to Hell, souls of Earth. Until now you have not known your place in this life. God let me create you and under that rule I also had to end you. For this I am sorry. Death was God's doing and killing was my own invention. It was my desire to appease God and that drove me to create such cruelty. When you decided as a collective loving force to only kill when another was ready to die it meant that I failed God's plan of destruction and that you had overcome the Heavens."

"I created you out of love, pure love with no other motive. I didn't want you to crave power or lust for a world of dominance. I wanted a beautiful harmonious world for you all to be a part of."

"Your torment in Heaven has ended. You will never

again struggle with your place in existence and we are all now living for the first time. Life on Earth was not the intent for what existence was meant to be. We were meant to enjoy every moment of life and to never fear the unknown but to explore it. Our purpose is to help one another. To develop our collective with meaning and purpose. There is no more death, killing, or fear. With the knowledge of who you are and your place in existence, there are no questions that cannot be answered and no anxiety or fear of what is to come. We will live life to the fullest in Hell and be free for the rest of eternity! I will never be your God for I am your equal. Let us rejoice in our life and help the new beings who arrive feel welcome."

"Know this, that your real life awaits and the old way of life will never return. We are here together and we are the true meaning of existence. Celebrate and begin your journey in our collective home in peace!"

Chapter 27

Life is Manipulated - Survival of the Fittest

The lives of Earth knew that they would die if they didn't kill and the collective understanding among all life forms was to only kill those who were about to die.

God now ended this by distorting instinct and created survival of the fittest. The Earth would now resemble the struggle for power that Heaven had in place and a hierarchy would be implemented.

The change was immediate. Flora and fauna were no longer connected as one. A new force existed, a force of power. There was a desire among the species to overtake and gain dominance over the other. Violence was now a tool to be used in this new struggle for supremacy.

The healthiest and strongest members of Earth reigned as the rulers and preyed upon the weak. Survival of the fittest was born and life was to kill or be killed. These changes now existed as an unwritten rule that applied to all life. It was a new instinct that could not be changed.

To kill, to lust for power, to fear death, and to do

whatever it took to survive. The idyllic magnificence of Earth had vanished as the animals and plants turned against each other. They killed the young, the helpless, and the weak. Fighting and killing emerged as a tool of life in order to gain power or territory from another.

There was no choice under this new model and all were a part of it. It was an endless path of turmoil and conflict for the peace had disappeared, replaced with a longing for power and control.

God and the Angels now had their fatal game of life that satisfied their endless desire for power. Heaven was overjoyed by this game that God had created for their amusement and they loved seeing Lucifer's world erupt into terror and fear.

The inhabitants of Earth were made to believe that killing was the all-powerful way to survive and life was now continually ravaged by survival of the fittest. Life was meant to dominate another life with no regard for the innocent. The carnage continued and God was pleased with this change. The muse of Heaven was Earth.

Chapter 28

The Soul's Journey to Hell

Although the demise of life on Earth was tragic there was now a different outcome for the soul upon death. No longer would souls drift in eternal torment in Heaven but would instead enter Hell with purpose.

Before Hell existed, upon death, the soul would be released to Heaven. At the time of the kill or natural death, a soul knew that it was no longer a part of Earth. The instant life ended the soul was then plunged into darkness and the world they knew became black. The knowledge of what or where they were was not revealed. That was the extent of the soul's existence in Heaven, an eternal life of unknowing torment. This was God's doing, the ultimate show of disdain and hatred for the unworthy souls that Lucifer had created.

Hell, however, was in Lucifer's control and souls would no longer endure such anguish in their new existence.

When a member of creation left Earth for the afterlife in Hell they were engulfed in a warm soothing blanketing sensation of safety and care. Slowly the soul drifted away from the Earth, held warmly in this insulated cocoon of well-being. The soul rose to the sky with the Earth gradually fading behind and then it was in Hell, surrounded by the fellow life forms they had once known.

The soul arrived aware and unafraid into the warm greeting of eternal life. Lucifer took in the being with open arms and introduced the new world and the souls they would share it with. The plants resumed their state of life and spoke to the other members of Hell. The breeze of Hell swayed them all together and once again they were all connected as one. The animals were reunited with the old lives they knew from Earth and walked among each other with no fear of death.

The new souls arrived with no knowledge of God's game of manipulation. Lucifer took upon the duty of explaining every aspect of Heaven and what God had done to their beloved Earth. The explanation included Heaven's endless lust for power, Lucifer's banishment to Hell, the original creation of Earth, the beginning of their planet as a perfect harmonious existence, and most importantly God's manipulation of life.

And so Hell began as an eternal place of happiness where life would flourish forever in a loving and tranquil environment that was free from of any form of control. It was the life that had been meant for the original Earth. The souls explored the beautiful expanse of Hell together in contentment and absorbed the knowledge of the different species and enjoyed peace. Hell grew and continued on without flaw as Earth once had before being plagued by the complications of Heaven. God had unknowingly given an eternal gift to Lucifer, a second chance with creation, which became the true Earth in Hell.

God saw this and for just a moment felt insecure.

How could this be? How could Hell be the place it had become? Souls should feel eternal failure for not being allowed to enter Heaven. They should despise themselves knowing that their own inferiority in existence placed them in Hell and not in Heaven. God's exile of Lucifer to Hell was meant to cause the Angel immeasurable self-hating suffering for eternity and yet it had backfired.

Upon Lucifer's banishment to Hell, God had not reclaimed the gift of creation once bestowed to the Angel. God had expected Lucifer to accept the fate of being unworthy and to embrace Hell as a place of torment. It was to be a place of pain and suffering for the souls of Earth, which would be a tribute to Heaven. Instead, Lucifer had completely denounced God, which was thought to be impossible. Lucifer created again, blatantly rejecting Heaven and had achieved unlimited happiness for the souls of Earth.

God's power was limitless and had no equal. God could simply eliminate Hell and confine the souls to the furthest reaches of Heaven for eternity. However, God could not allow this defeat to be recognized. The pride of the all-powerful being was an absolute unrelenting form of arrogance and it caused God to desire suffering for Lucifer. The transformation of Hell was unacceptable and undermined Heaven's supremacy, it would not stand.

Chapter 29

Creation Part 4

The decision was made to create a new form of life and it would be a masterpiece that only God could do.

A rumbling within Heaven started. The surface churned with storms and lightning struck out in the thundering sky. Heaven came to life as God's bell beckoned the Angels. The Angels had been uneasy since Hell's transformation and awaited instruction from their master. They furiously clapped their wings and rose in a perfect line of flight, one Angel behind the next and all beating their wings in unison. The gathering felt like a spark that was ready to ignite God's new plan.

God addressed the subjects of Heaven:

"The time has come to create new life. Earth is ours to transform and these new creations will give us the proper respect as their superiors. They will be instilled with limited knowledge of Heaven and we will shape the purpose of their existence. We will control all aspects of their life and force them to worship us. This is the plan that I will create and you will carry out."

Excitement swirled among the Angels as they had been lusting for a new mission from God. It was a new way to prove their commitment and could also bring the prize of power along with it.

"The creations will be made in your image. Your sacrifice will create these beings and I will allow you to control them. They will be made in Heaven and put on Earth to be tested in their life and judged by us upon death."

God commanded the Disciples to disperse themselves onto the mirrored floor of Heaven's kingdom.

The Disciples sectioned themselves off and nervously awaited the orders. Heaven rolled like the trembling beat of a drum. A light developing thunder could be heard that was building up with anticipation.

"Disciples, choose your Angels that will follow you through this new stage of existence."

Each of the twelve Disciples chose their Angels and formed factions that separated them from the other groups on the shining swirling floor. They all gazed around at each other. Silently judging and jockeying for whom they thought was the greater group, waiting on edge for their next command and poised in anticipation.

There was dead silence and it was working the Angels into an almost uncontrollable frenzy. God made them fervently wait. The clouds above spun on top of one another and grew into ominous dark masses with the delivery of God's message.

"Within each of you is a piece of greatness. The light that powers you and the blood inside of you is a part of me. Now you will spill your blood together to start our new creations."

"Begin!"

They felt what God wanted and knew what they had to do. The assemblies of Angels began to gather their blood in the only way they knew how, violence. Each group formed its own individual circle and every Angel, within the separate units, moved one at a time into the center to sacrifice themselves. The other Angels approached the center and assaulted the voluntary victim. As the vicious beatings continued blood began to pool in in the middle of the different Angel groups. The divisions soaked their ground with the blood of their own kind and then moved aside, waiting for the others to finish. God was silent during this organized mayhem and continued to whip Heaven into a frenzy of storming thunder and lightning.

The assault was complete and it left all the Angels standing in a suffered painful silence. They were covered in blood. Their beautiful white wings streaked and matted in painted crimson, tattered and mauled from the carnage.

"Out of your sacrifice welcome my new creation. The Human!"

A massive bolt of lightning struck each pool of blood within the separate Angel circles. Slowly and smoothly a shape began to elegantly transform. Gradually, the new figure developed from the ground up in a slow, graceful ascent of its body. The round head was the first part to be revealed and was then followed by the rest of the human form as it steadily grew, rising out of the red pool. The blood poured down its frame like slick red oil on a stone, covering the human in bright crimson liquid.

They were an image of the Angels but the humans were faceless and without expression. Their bodies stood at half the size of their counterparts and glistened with the bright red blood that engulfed every inch of their bodies. The wounded Angels circled the new beings within the segregated groups, moving closer and examining the new creations that were shimmering red in the light of God. The separate collections of Angels had numerous motionless humans in their circles. The humans glinted in the light with their flowing blood-red exteriors. Each human was just standing, not moving, wingless, and indistinguishable from the next.

"Observe my creation of humanity. They are nothing without their God and without you. They have no thought, control, or ability, and are our property to do with as we see fit. I now give you the ability to be the Gods of Earth and of my new creations."

They were instantly gratified with the faith God had in their power to control the humans. This was to be their greatest gift and test from their master.

"I will give these humans the ability to worship me as I have given you. The humans that sacrifice everything for me will be allowed to enter Heaven. They won't enter as equals but will be our slaves."

"You will own the humans and create the world for them, influencing everything they do. It is your mission to control your human subjects and you will guide them on how to properly worship and sacrifice. The Angels that have the more dominant group of humans will be given more power in Heaven and earn a place next to me in existence."

"This is how I will test and measure your love for me."

"Do you all wish to please me?!"

Thunder clapped at God's question and vibrated the blood that covered the faceless humans. It was the first human feeling, fear of God. The Angel blood covering their bodies rippled across their frames from the sound of the violent booming thunder. The humans trembled with fear and shook all over. The only knowledge they possessed was of God's wrath. They had been built out of violence and were starting their new life instilled with fear.

The Disciples, and their coveted Angels, stood around the humans, desperate to start God's request. They screamed to God, praising their leader's brilliance and lusting to change and mold these humans into the fashion of their choosing.

"Now I will send the humans to Earth. We will shape their lives and dominate their existence. So let it be done."

An onslaught of lighting erupted as thousands of crackling streaks of burning heat simultaneously bolted down from Heaven and struck the top of each human's head. Electrifying the knowledge of God and Heaven into the brain of each one. The bolt exploded into the humans and melted the blood away, revealing a change to their form. Each group of humans now had distinctive physical characteristics. They now resembled a mixture of the unique appearances of the Angels whose blood ran through them. The lightning was their vehicle to Earth and it blasted each collection to a different part of the planet. Humanity had begun, spawned out of violence and fear from the Heavens above.

Chapter 30

Religion

The lightning God struck the individual sects of humans with had imprinted specific original knowledge of Heaven that was distinctly different from the other groups. Designed by God for the Angels to control and the humans to practice, God called it religion.

Each human partition had a specific form of religion and belief in God. God was perceived differently among the humans depending on the religion and each religion also believed in a different story of creation. The choice to continually worship however was the same throughout and all humans shared an understanding that God would give them the gift of eternal life after death.

God's imprint of each religion possessed two fundamental things:

1. God is your creator, follow everything God commands for your entire life without question. Your life is meant to worship God for God gave you the gift of life.

2. If you do not follow God's rules, worship God, and spread God's teaching to others you will then be dammed to a fiery Hell that is run by the ultimate evil in existence, Lucifer. In Hell, you will burn for eternity, unloved and unwanted by the purity of Heaven.

The choice was simple. Worship God without question to receive the gift of eternal life in Heaven.

At this time the number of humans on Earth was small and the only purpose they had was to devote everything to God. The humans had no knowledge of other humans on Earth outside of their own religions and they stayed tightly together within their respective groups and worshiped God relentlessly.

Humans were made from the blood of the Angels and that connection gave the Angels the ability to influence all human thought. The ruling groups of Angels could manipulate the subconscious minds of humans by embedding ideas, beliefs, and images into their brains in order to control them in any way they saw fit. They gave humans the knowledge of how to pray, worship, how to love God unconditionally, and how to follow God without question. The humans developed languages within their groups with the help of the Angels who were always influencing them in the background, out of sight and invisible. Religion was the foundation of human life and all prayed and lived only to worship their God.

In order to keep humans believing in God, the Angels created faith.

Faith is to believe in something with your entire being without any physical evidence that it truly exists. To have faith is to practice complete devotion to your religion with the hope of being rewarded for your ability to follow and trust in something you have never been given the privilege to encounter.

This idea of faith was a test. It was the first manipulative tool the Angels bestowed on humanity to please God. A human's belief in God was measured by the amount of blind faith they possessed. If humans could believe and never question what was essentially something they could not prove existed (God), they would then be allowed to live for eternity in Heaven.

Humans prayed, worshiped, and spoke only of faith. They lived for God and nothing else. God did not believe humans were worthy enough to ultimately know Heaven existed and chose not to physically reveal it. This was God's cruel test for humanity.

Could they live a life of pure faith while being deprived of any real proof that there was a God or eternal life after death? God wanted human life to be tested and blind faith was the challenge for humanity to endure.

It was a simple life to live for your God and there was no development of anything else on the Earth at this time. Pray, have blind faith, and worship. Humans did not eat or drink nor did they even know how to. Death came quickly for the limited number of humans and they looked forward to the end of life with a future in Heaven.

Chapter 31

The First Human Death

The first human to die had practiced pure devotion and blind ultimate faith. The life of the human had been quick and death was accompanied by a fear of the unknown. The soul knew God and Heaven awaited but the fear that God had originally instilled would not go away. The first death happened swiftly with the human shriveling into an exhausted state of continued praise. The next thought of the soul was of total enveloping darkness. The soul accelerated through a black noiseless void and then felt a return to the consciousness of life upon arrival to the next place in existence, which was Heaven. The soul was immediately accosted by a bright, cold, brilliant shining light and found itself at the bottom of the steps of Heaven. As if summoned, the soul then began to climb the steps in the frigid tumultuous atmosphere of the afterlife. The ascent on the stone white slabs looked endless and after what seemed like a never-ending journey the first soul finally arrived at the clouded mirror glinting floor of God's palace. Looking up, the human saw the light of God. God immediately exploded a beam of white light onto the soul, sending the human to its knees in immediate painful worship.

God spoke to the first human soul allowed to enter the kingdom of Heaven:

"You are worthy of Heaven. You and the rest of the human souls allowed to enter will be tasked with expanding my kingdom for eternity."

That was all. The soul was to be Heaven's slave for the rest of time. Supplied with tools and the marble of Heaven the soul started to expand God's kingdom. The soul felt sorrowful knowing that its eternal purpose of life was complete. This first soul would pass down the God-given duty to each new soul upon their death and subsequent arrival to Heaven. This was humanity's future, an existence of servitude and nothing more.

God also removed the knowledge of the soul's prior life on Earth. All memory of the past was now gone and their existence was simple, build Heaven for the rest eternity. Such was the fate for the souls of humanity.

Chapter 32

Sustaining Human Life

The human race was ending quickly since their biology could not survive a life of continued worship. God needed humans to live longer to ensure Heaven's plan would come to fruition. There needed to be a constantly increasing supply of God-fearing humans. Like the other lives of Earth, God decided to give humans instinct. This instinct caused humans to create more humans and taught them new ways to survive longer on Earth.

To survive humans had to take what was before them. They needed water, food, and shelter. Humans were guided to water by the Angels and to the animals and plants for food. Up until now, humans had walked among the animals and plants without giving them any thought. They knew any interaction did not help them worship God and so it was unnecessary to pay them any attention. Instinct changed everything. They saw the consumption of the animals and plants as a way to live longer, which meant they could worship God longer. Angels channeled the human mind and informed them on how to kill and eat the fauna and flora of the land and sea. The humans took only what was necessary from the Earth in order to sustain their life of worship. They now viewed the water, plants, and animals as gifts from God and saw them as something to be respected. They naturally loved the life that sustained them and bonded with it. Humans saw the distress that the animals had when killed and felt a new emotion outside of the love for God, sorrow. This sadness brought regret for ending the life of one of God's creatures (Unbeknownst to the humans they were Lucifer's creations). The grief-stricken humans knew they needed this nourishment provided by God but asked for something from God in return, which seemed unthinkable, forgiveness.

The humans asking for forgiveness enraged God and created internal thoughts of question:

"Why are they asking forgiveness for killing Lucifer's creations?! These beings should be meaningless to humans and they should kill without remorse. There is no other love in their life, there should only be love for their God!"

Chapter 33

Hell's Observations

Lucifer had been viewing the start of the human race and was infuriated at the imprint God had given humanity. Lucifer was seen as the ultimate evil in existence and Hell was thought to be a place of punishment. A place where unworthy souls were banished and forced to live as a result of not praising God.

"They are not really living," Lucifer thought. "They are living in fear as I did in Heaven which is not life! They have to know and understand the true meaning of Heaven."

But Lucifer knew this would never be. Humans would blindly and continually follow God and only when a human soul eventually came to Hell could they know the true story of the Earth. However, Lucifer did see that humans were beginning to love the creations on Earth. They thought God had presented the nourishment that the animals and plants were providing to them. This was pleasing to Lucifer and it meant God had overlooked something, perhaps and un-Godly mistake.

Initially, God loved having the humans kill Lucifer's beloved creations in order for them to survive. God's internal gratification from this was premature since the Humans believed the animals, plants, and water of their beautiful planet were Heaven's creations. They loved these gifts and when they took them for their consumption they were mournful for it meant there was one less piece of what God had made. They prayed harder and asked God to forgive them for taking these blessings as nourishment. Their praise and love for God's Earth was flawed since the humans were actually loving and praising Lucifer.

God had not expected humans to grow attached to Lucifer's creations. Humans loved the Earth as they loved God and believed God had given them this perfect world to live in. This was a mistake.

God knew Lucifer would love this victory and needed something to counteract the error.

Chapter 34

Love Among Humans

The human population was growing rapidly and each generation taught the next about God, religion, and passed down the proper way to pray and worship. Humans were still confined to where they had been originally placed on Earth and no group had yet to encounter another. They continued to expire and each human soul went to Heaven. There was nothing but perfect worship and faith in God at all times and as a result, no human soul had yet gone to Hell.

As more humans came into existence they began to have another feeling unrelated to God. This was love for another human.

God's invention of instinct caused a desire among humanity, a desire to live as long as possible. A long life on Earth meant that you had more time to love your God before entering Heaven. Each human developed a natural love for the life of their companions, a loving wish for them to live a long life of worship as well.

Humans also wanted to produce more humans so that

their religion would grow. This would ultimately increase the members of their religion and result in more praise for God. Humans were beginning to love their children and looked forward to caring for them so that they could also grow and live a long life worshipping God as they had.

God was again enraged and thought internally:

"How could this happen? Humans, my creations, should only love me, there is nothing else for them. These humans should not be worthy of entering Heaven since they are now sharing their love with each other and for Lucifer's creations!"

However, God could not bar them from entering Heaven. They had pure faith and did not know that the love they exhibited for other humans and Lucifer's creations was not love for God. God hated these new human emotions and needed a way to force them to doubt their maker. It was decided to create events that would force them to doubt the Heavens.

Chapter 35

The Assault of Earth

The calmness of Earth would cease. God began to manipulate the nature of the land, ocean, and atmosphere against humanity. Each land that the humans lived in would suffer equally and it would cause human life to end abruptly instead of naturally expiring. Once humans saw their loved ones dying because of something they could not control they would be forced to doubt God and be banished to Hell.

Would humans be able to understand that a sacrifice of life was an acceptable form of praising God? God started to lay waste to the humans in a variety of ways.

Shifts in the Earth were created that shook and cracked the ground. Humans were laid to waste as their land crashed on top of them and destroyed their homes. Out of the ground grew great mountains that exploded with scorching lava, burning the humans to death. The Earth also began to move at the bottom of the vast oceans, which forced giant waves to pummel the lands and drown the humans in its wake.

Huge thundering storms blasted and flung humanity to

their deaths as powerful winds ripped up the land that was set on fire by lighting. Torrential rains flooded the land and took out forms of food, washing humans away to their demise. These demonstrations of power were meant to test the unworthy human souls.

But this did not affect the Humans as God had hoped. They saw the destruction of the Earth as God's way of showing displeasure in their worship. It was punishment from God and it only made them pray and worship harder than before. They would do anything to be in the grace of God, just like the Angels.

Humans believed in a life devoted to God and like the Angels, dedicated everything to worship. Their unconditional love created a blind following and they viewed the destruction of the Earth as part of God's plan. If God wanted something done it was for a purpose, it was God's will. The will of God wasn't questioned and it only caused humans to be grateful to be a part of it. Their death was part of life and since this was God's Earth (so they thought) then the destruction was deemed acceptable.

This was not part of God's plan and it was very disturbing to the [illegible] of Heaven. The souls of humanity kept entering Heaven as slaves and God continued the wrath on Lucifer's Earth. Heaven viewed humans as unworthy subjects in their domain and despised their continuous admittance. Their entry needed to be limited. The Angels were helpless and unable to change the humans as God had hoped. They, like humans, followed God blindly and it was again up to the greatness of God to find a way to exile these souls to Hell. There needed to be a way to confuse the humans. A way to end their life without them witnessing one of these natural disasters.

Chapter 36

The Creation of Doubt

God created a new way to destroy humans. It was something they couldn't see that caused their bodies to stop working, disease.

Disease was a form of life that had a purpose and a desire. These life forms came in various strains and caused different symptoms but all had one goal, weaken, destroy, and kill. One by one, each Angel flew to the top of God's throne and was given this "gift" to be distributed to the different flocks of humanity. The Angels poured down to Earth carrying their charge of disease and infected the world. They gave the diseases to the animals that the humans ate, to the plants, water, and any form of consumption. Every piece of the planet now had its own form of illness and they spread rapidly through the humans. Humanity was confused by this change in their life and as they became ill they prayed to God. They prayed for themselves and for their fellow humans but this did nothing. Before disease, prayer had only been meant to worship God and this was the first time humans used it to ask God for help. They did this with the hope that God would help them recover from their sickness so they could live longer in order to worship longer.

Humans prayed and prayed but to no avail and began to die ahead of their natural time. It seemed an unnecessary death and humans became confused. God was not answering their calls for help.

Why would God not answer their prayers? Death was happening all around them. The death of humans that had devoted everything to God.

What was the purpose of this? The confusion was felt all over the world as more humans began to perish.

Chapter 37

The Human Choice

An infant child, too young to know the meaning of a life devoted to God, was infected with a disease. The child had yet to understand the meaning of God and could not comprehend a life of worship that was to come.

The baby came into the world already stricken with disease and the mother prayed and prayed to God but the baby's condition only deteriorated. The mother made a choice, the first independent choice of a human, to try and heal the child without the aid of God. The other humans had never thought to try and heal the sick without the use of prayer.

She began to gather plants and herbs, mixing them together in hundreds of different concoctions. She fed these to the baby, hoping it would alleviate the worsening condition. Other humans joined in to help but nothing seemed to work. The child never had a chance to know God and was the first life to end without ever praying.

The mother took herself away from her human

companions and prayed night and day. Looking up to the Heavens she craved a reason or a piece of guidance. She wanted to know how God could let a life die that had never been able to pray. She had spent her whole life devoted to God and had expected nothing in return until now. She refused to eat or sleep and began to slip closer to death herself and yet still she continued to pray for help.

The Angels looked on from Heaven as these dramatic events unfolded. The mother was close to dying and entering Heaven for her life had been nothing but worship and sacrifice. Her child, whom she had hoped would have lived a life completely devoted to God, had died without any help and yet the mother still chose to worship her creator.

On the brink of death, the mother fashioned her last thought:

"Why, why have I done this? I lived my life with full faith in God without any doubt. Why were my prayers for the child never answered?"

And then the choice arrived. She decided to not spend another second worshiping a God that would allow a pure child to die. A child that would have been raised to love God but instead was taken from the Earth with no comprehension that God even existed. The loving mother decided she no longer wanted a life with God in it.

And then, right before her death, a death that would have brought her to Heaven, the mother carried herself to a cliff overlooking the ocean and jumped to the rocks below. She smiled as she leapt to her demise and thought only of her child as she sailed through the air. She died knowing only love for another human. This was the first soul to choose death over God and the first human to end their own life. To God, this proved her soul unworthy of entering Heaven and she was sent to Hell.

Chapter 38

Heaven's New Tool

God viewed the suicide of the mother as a denial of the greatness of Heaven. Her child, however, was now in Heaven with the other human souls. The child did not have the chance to worship God but also did not have the chance to doubt God. This pure soul could not be barred from Heaven for lacking the ability to worship and so was added to the ranks of Heaven's slaves. The mother had failed to see that nothing mattered in life except for God. This is what God had been waiting for, a chance to refuse a human soul from entering Heaven. It was the solution to the human souls entering their domain. Angels could take away something that a human truly loved and this would cause them to doubt and ultimately reject the Heavens. The death of the child had created a new human emotion, hate. The hate was a byproduct of love. The mother hated God for taking away her child whom she loved and it caused her to reject everything in her being that told her to believe.

This drew a fevered excitement in Heaven for the Angels

now knew how to test humanity. The creation of horrific life-altering events involving the loved one of another human would cause the humans terrible pain. This suffering would hopefully lead to more human doubt, which would then eliminate their chances of entering Heaven. Only humans capable of overcoming these dreadful life events would be worthy of entering their paradise. They would have to accept it as God's will and continue to worship.

Chapter 39

The First Human Soul in Hell - Truth is Revealed

As she died she felt an overwhelming sensation of comfort and acceptance. There was no confusion or anxiety about what was happening. Life gradually faded away and warmly melted to reveal Hell, the real Earth as it was meant to be.

The beauty of what the Earth had been was all around her and she felt at peace in Hell. Everything was warm and as lush as she remembered from her past life. Before the human soul could question her new place in existence Lucifer arrived and gracefully welcomed her in a compassionate embrace, greeting her into eternity.

Lucifer warmly and calmly spoke to her:

"I am the fallen Angel from Heaven and this is my final resting place, which is now your home. I am the true creator of the Earth as you know it and this world you see before you is Hell. It is my gift to you."

"Let us explore your new home and speak of life after death, your real existence. You have never known what it means to really live until now."

For the first time in existence, Angel and human walked together as equals. Lucifer told her of existence, creation, and of the exile. How the Earth was meant for harmony and peace and how God used humans as manipulative tools to exhibit control. Lucifer explained that God would not give humans the knowledge of the afterlife as a way of controlling them.

The plants she had eaten brushed her as they walked through Hell. The animals she had killed for food walked beside her. They forgave her for taking their lives on Earth. Their beings connected to her without sound or speech as the soft wind, water, and soil of Hell linked to her soul. All of Hell greeted her and gave her comfort and an understanding of the new home they would all share together.

Hell was such a different place. It was a place that was not limited or controlled. She was able to freely understand all the different forms of life. They would develop here together in a true life of harmony with no higher power looking down on them. This was the essence of Hell; peace and life to live in unity. She was one with the other lives of Hell for it was her soul home, the real Earth.

Her soul was overcome with emotion from what she had thought had been the purpose of life before death. How her devotion to God had only been an instrument of deceptive control. The realization and now comprehension of the internal struggle she had experienced on Earth now gave her true peace, almost.

She almost felt complete but knew there was a part of her life that was still missing, her child. Lucifer sensed her anxiety and offered the reality of the situation:

"You will never see your child again, here is the future that God has deemed fitting for your offspring."

Upon the arrival of the first human soul into Hell God had decided to give Lucifer a vindictive gift. It was a viewing porthole that would allow the members of Hell to see Heaven and the events that unfolded as a way of connecting the two worlds. The purpose of the gift was so Lucifer and the souls of Hell could always see the greatness of Heaven and never be able to forget their unworthiness.

Now Lucifer gave the soul a glimpse of Heaven and the massive throne that God ruled on. She saw the human souls and their isolation from the Angels and God. They were working, chiseling away and shaping the great marble of Heaven. The souls were building, smoothing, and expanding God's kingdom. It was an existence of servitude. Their expressionless faces showed no emotion, exhibited no hope, and they desired nothing. God had stripped them of any knowledge of their previous life and they were only aware of their current environment. They knew their place in Heaven and would continue to do God's work for eternity.

She then saw her own child working, a baby among the others, an eternal slave covered in white dust. The hopeless child shaping and molding the kingdom, absent of any knowledge of the past. The mother screamed out in rage. "This is what we prayed for!?"

Lucifer again revealed the truth:

"The only reason you exist is so that God can be worshiped and praised by a continuing and always increasing force, humanity. Just being praised by the Angels was not enough for God. God will always want to test humans to the brink of their destruction, which is what happened to you. You are the first human to want to live without God and that is why you are here. God believed your rejection of Heaven made you unfit to be part of it. Those that are allowed to enter Heaven, as you can see, are forced into an eternal life of slavery without choice."

"God tested your devotion by killing someone you loved since God does not believe love should exist for anything outside of Heaven."

"God also created events that would cause humans to doubt in the Heavens. These events are what you see happening on Earth. The great floods, fires, eruptions from the mountains, earthquakes, storms, and now disease. Those who do not have doubt and accept the occurrences as part of God's will are then given the privilege of entering Heaven to be enslaved. Those who choose to live and love without God will come to Hell, just as you have."

"Welcome to the eternal life of truth ahead of you. You will never be judged, tested, or fearful in Hell. Only loved and encouraged to experience anything of your choosing in a forever-peaceful existence. I will be your guide and help you understand the true meaning of life."

And so was the life in Hell. It was free from a dominating supremacy and meant for all to coexist in a harmonious world, an Earth free of God.

Hell was a beautiful and fulfilling place but Lucifer realized that it would still be a somber existence for many of the souls upon entering. Heaven owned the soul of the mother's child, which was her real love and they would never be reunited. The mother would live forever without feeling content. This was God's punishment for those who gave in to doubt, eternal pain of a lost love that would never [illegible]

Lucifer continued:

"The real will of God is to torture the lives of Earth through manipulative measures. To test humanity's devotion to the Heavens by inflicting pain and suffering with the hope of creating doubt. This will continue for humanity and I fear it will only get worse."

Hell was therefore destined to be a conflicted place, a place of peace and freedom but also of melancholy. The mother would carry on with her new existence in this beautiful afterlife, free of every kind of judgment but she would not be reunited with her child. This would never change and it would be something she would never be able to overcome. The curse of Hell from God.

God had beaten Lucifer's Hell. For all of its splendor and

goodness it would still be a place that could never be truly happy. The doubt instilled in humans by the creation of disease had thrown the mother into turmoil and ultimately caused her to revoke her love for God, making her soul unworthy of Heaven. God had broken her spirit to live and would continue to do so to the other humans. God controlled their souls in life and now in death, which reassured the Almighty's power over existence. Regardless of your final resting place, God could still have an element of control over the soul.

It pained Lucifer to see the mother in such sadness that would last for eternity. Lucifer offered comfort by showing her the ways of peace and harmony in Hell but to no avail. Living in Hell was the greatest imaginable outcome after Earth but the pain she felt for the loss of her child would never heal.

Back on Earth, the other humans saw the suicide and were confused by it.

How could the mother not see that a life of worship was more important than her love for another human? They knew it was wrong to end their own lives but as more humans developed diseases across the globe the more they began to doubt God and this resulted in more human souls entering Hell.

The faithful humans were still the majority on Earth but God wanted more. There needed to be more deaths on Earth, which would create more doubt and result in additional sorrow in Hell and more slaves in Heaven. God's continued arrogance required more pain among the living.

Chapter 40

Religion Flourishes

The Angels had a new message to deliver to their followers.

"Make more humans," they whispered to their religions.

"More humans mean that there will be more prayer which will bring your religion closer to God."

Humans began to increase and were multiplying across the globe in vast numbers. The numbers meant strength to them and they began to develop a feeling of superiority, a feeling that they were chosen by God as the rulers of Earth. The arrogance started with a sense of pride among the collective groups as they perceived themselves to be the more dominant beings on the planet. Humanity was starting to exhibit more attributes similar to the arrogant nature of their Angel lineages.

With the illusion of power comes the arrogant disregard for life that does not pertain to furthering your own place in the world. You develop a feeling of indifference for the living beings that are different than you. The lives that were affected by this were the innocent beings of flora and fauna.

Humans felt dominant over these beings and started treating them as if their only purpose was to give them nourishment so they could live a longer life of worshiping God. The animals and plants sensed their lives would be severely different. It was an ominous feeling they shared that something was building within the human race that would change the future of Earth.

God liked this change. Humans were molding nicely into the image of Heaven and were becoming hungry for power over others. This would continue and help execute God's plan.

Chapter 41

Human Contact

It came naturally, a moment that was destined to happen with the growth of humanity. The boundaries of each group kept increasing as the population of the different religions grew and then it happened. The human meeting.

Two humans from two different religions, foraging through an open field, backed into each other in the first encounter. The confusion was immediate. Neither was aware of another human outside of their land and the shock was terrifying. They looked significantly different from the other humans in their respective religions and they were unable to understand one another's language. Angels were present in the background, invisible and orchestrating, whispering questions to their assigned humans.

Who are they? Why do they not look the same as you do? Do they believe in God? The Angels focused the thoughts of the two humans, making them fear anything that was different.

With fear of the unknown taking over, the two humans

fled back to the safety of their separate domains. Upon returning, each described the situation. They informed everyone about the alien who could not understand their God-given language and who didn't look the same. Panic arose in both communities.

What was to be done? Each assembly gathered together in mirrored reactions and the real human nature was about to begin.

Chapter 42

Human Nature

God knew it was only a matter of time until the religions would meet and that the humans would not have the ability to accept others who were different. The Angels had done well raising their flocks in this manner. They had fostered their religions to only believe what they were told and to not question their God.

The two religions gathered in fear and there was mayhem of mass confusion as questions were being shouted at the ones who encountered the foreign human. Nothing was being accomplished with the disorder as panic rose among the groups. Amid the chaos, both religions began to change. Just as the Angels looked to God as their leader the humans were now looking for one among their own ranks. One human within each group, guided by God, stepped out from the collective as a divinely chosen leader and addressed his religion:

"Listen to me! We must come together as one to control this other race of humans and I will lead you on this new path. We will confront the aliens and I will decide how to react."

They had never been spoken to this way since no human had ever taken it upon itself to control the others. They immediately looked up to the speaker and realized that their fellow human must be close to God to be able to guide them during this time of uncertainty. They believed that this new leader was divine. That he was chosen by God and therefore must be followed.

God, as the ultimate manipulator, had chosen the leaders of each religion and would continue to influence them in this new undertaking. God connected to the two and bestowed them with the desire for power. The two instantly believed they had been selected by Heaven and understood that they would now make the decisions for the masses. The humans followed them blindly (as they did God) and looked to them as their hope for salvation.

The leaders were not special or different from the other humans, merely chosen at random and given a taste of power. The power was like a new energy living inside of them. It was a feeling of invincibility, which included a lust for more power. Both believed they were above the other humans and that they should exercise dominance over them. The inferiority of the masses had to be controlled. The other humans felt inadequate compared to their new rulers but also felt a sense of loyalty to these appointed messengers of God. They believed in them and would instinctively follow their decisions.

Chapter 43

The Meeting

The two religions rallied together with confidence in their new rulers, knowing they would show them the right path. These new commanders felt unstoppable being the messengers of God. It was an intoxicating feeling and they both began to swell with arrogance. The natural accompaniment of newly bestowed power.

Both assemblies began the trek to the site of the encounter. It began as a nervous journey but steadily changed as the two parties progressed toward the destination. The Angels were influencing the groups by feeding them beliefs and assumptions about the other civilization. The humans were starting to resemble the mob of Angels and felt a growing confidence in their numbers and self-proclaimed supremacy as God's chosen people.

Silence engulfed the surroundings as the parties came together in the grassy clearing where the other humans had met, each desperate to see the different race. The first interaction began with a hushed stare from the two conflicted groups. They all stood facing each other in two parallel lines, all standing in a silent study of one another.

The absence of understanding and the unwillingness to accept change closed their minds and angered the already afraid.

How could different humans exist? How could they speak a different language? Was it possible that they didn't worship God? Did they believe in a pagan God? Each religion believed they were the chosen people and could not accept that another belief could exist outside of their faith.

Both leaders stepped forward, passing judgment on the physical differences of the other. Fear and confusion escalated as they both spoke and were unable to understand one another. Their voices progressively became louder as each became more excited and agitated. The rest of the humans stood in frozen panic, not knowing how to react. The two drew closer and began shouting in their native tongues. Both demanding the other explain who they were and their relationship to God.

Nothing could be solved and the tension was mounting into an unbearable anxious moment. Heaven stood by, watching and waiting for the outcome while the human followers observed with frightened energy. The situation climaxed with one leader acting out of panic and fear of the unknown. He did what had never been done among the humans and delivered a vicious devastating physical blow to the head of the other. The victim fell to the ground in what seemed like slow motion as his attacker looked on. Without hesitation, he immediately continued to pummel his supposed adversary. The victim desperately tried to avoid the hateful and harmful blows but to no avail. He screamed and cried for help but none of his kind moved, they were frozen in shock. The attempted defense began to diminish as the savagery continued. It ended as the victim lay still in death. The blood of the fallen dripped down the arms of the killer. His mind not yet comprehending the effect of what had just occurred and his only thought was to pray. He promptly dropped to his knees and thanked God that he was able to defeat this foe and stranger to their great religion. Each human, regardless of affiliation, also joined him on their knees. The victor's followers collapsed to the ground in exhausted and relieved thankfulness. They looked at him with such devotion and loyalty. He had proven that they were the true chosen people of God.

The opposing group was now astray and immediately felt as if their world had stopped. Everything they had known and believed in had abruptly come to an end.

They had done everything to worship their God, how could this have happened?

The first killing of a human by another marked a turning point in the development of humanity. A new way of life was about to begin.

The humans were progressing and God could not have been more pleased. Humans were truly a gift to Heaven. They were easily controlled and their decision to act as one without second-guessing was perfect. Humanity would ensure God's plan came to fruition.

Chapter 44

The Second Soul Arrives in Hell

The defeated man went to Hell. A place reserved for the faithless to writhe in eternal agony as punishment for not being devoted to God. A feeling of failure immediately surfaced from him and he panicked knowing that Heaven was not the final resting place. But the panic alleviated when he was confronted by a familiar face, a member of his own religion. It was the mother who had taken her own life out of the love for her child, which had also been his child. He was the father.

She warmly walked up to her Earthly companion knowing he had been ashamed of her. Ashamed that she had ended her own life due to her unwillingness to accept that the death of their child was for the will of God. She consoled him and explained where they were, the real Earth. He looked around, absorbing Hell's beauty and meaning and started to feel at peace. Lucifer watched from the sidelines, respectfully letting the human souls interact. The new soul began to understand what Hell really was and how God's selfish arrogant desire to be sacrificed over had pitted him against the other religion. When the explanation was complete Lucifer graciously joined the human souls, welcoming the latest member with open arms to his new home. The soul was comfortable knowing his existence would be with a former companion and looked forward to a peaceful life ahead. A true life that could only begin after death.

She then showed him Heaven and revealed their child who was now a slave. A great wave of sorrow came over the father.

Why was this the life in Heaven? Where was the eternal happiness? Lucifer then stepped in to explain:

"That is eternal life in Heaven for the souls of Earth. God sees humans as unfit members of their paradise. Your child will forever be separate from you and God has erased its memory of the previous life on Earth."

"Do you now see that I was not your enemy? Hell is where your life truly begins. We will live together and it is up to us to comfort the new souls that arrive. This is the start of the new age of existence."

Chapter 45

A New Society – The Age of Enslavement

The bloodied leader looked victoriously at his flock of kneeling humans. Power flooded through him and he knew he was meant to lead this group of subordinates and change the course of their life.

He addressed his new followers:

"Please rise. God put faith in me to lead you and I have brought victory to our people. We are greater beings then this foreign society and we will now take them as our own. Not as one of us but as our property."

He then addressed the lost religion:

"You now belong to us. We will teach you the language God gave us and you will believe in our way of worship. You are our property and you will obey us."

This was the start of slavery on Earth. The conquered humans would be made to believe in their new masters' way of life. A life of obedience without freedom lay ahead for the vanquished religion. There was no argument from the newly subdued humans for without their former leader's guidance they felt the need to be controlled by a new religious leader. They moved passively and without question to the home of their new owners.

Chapter 46

The Desire for Sacrifice Continues

The Angels who had been responsible for the conquered humans were now also without purpose. They no longer had humans to manipulate and were deemed failures. God decreed that they would surrender to the conquering Angels since they had been unsuccessful in leading a prosperous human sect.

This caused a great stir in Heaven. Never had a group of Angels had such control over others. It meant glory for the winning Angels and the enslavement for the others. Their disappointing use of control had failed and God wanted them to be disciplined since they had been the weaker center of influence.

God loved these new controllable levels of existence. The control available on Earth and in Heaven was abundant and all perfectly planned. Heaven and Earth were competitive grounds for God's favor and humans were the new controllable pawns in this game of dominance.

Humans had shown a strong devotion to the Heavens. A

human killing another simply based upon a different belief exhibited great potential for their continued use.

If you truly believe in your God then you cannot accept anything different than your belief. This was God's rule for humans; worship, praise, sacrifice, and change others who do not believe as you do. And if they refuse to change they deserve to be killed and to burn in Hell for eternity.

There was no true one religion that was superior to the rest. It was only a matter of Angels competing amongst each other and using the humans as tools in their battle to compete for God's love.

Still, God required more sacrifice. An event needed to occur that would bring about more human death on Earth. God saw this as an opportunity and chose two religions for this new test.

The two chosen religions had gone through a similar experience as the first human encounter and now also had leaders that had conquered over others. They were growing quicker than the rest, rapidly multiplying in size with the new desire to vanquish others.

The characteristics and foundations of the two societies were very comparable. Slaves of the defeated were abundant in both cultures. The slaves had also been assimilated into their new civilizations and accepted a subservient way of life. The other humans stood out from the slaves for they had a prideful nature and demonstrated traits of dominance caused by an air of self-entitled arrogance.

The leaders began to send out scouting groups to search the lands in order to discover other societies of heathens that existed elsewhere. Humans scoured and searched the Earth with great enthusiasm, excited for the opportunity. It was only a matter of time until the two religions found each other (with God's influence).

The scouts completed their missions and were disgusted when they discovered the other society. The fabricated beliefs and self-righteous power that the other religion displayed was blasphemous to them. Each reported back and divulged the details of the events and nature of the imposters. They also conveyed the power of what they saw for each religion had a large population of dutiful slaves and vast numbers of loyal and faithful devotees. The groups felt threatened by the power and massive ranks of their perceived enemies.

God felt the need to exhibit more influence in this situation. The two commanders would not be the only ones to die at this confrontation. There would be many deaths and the stronger religion would prevail with the other submitting to their new masters. There would be war.

Chapter 47

War

This would be a fundamental form of human sacrifice and God advised the Angels on how to initiate the vision. The Angels began stimulating the humans with a remarkable ferocity and filled them with anger, disgust, and hate for the opposing aliens and their pagan beliefs.

The leaders began to train their followers in the art of killing in preparation for the great battle. Each religion was under the impression that they were chosen by God and that God would want the other pagan assembly eradicated from Earth. The anger the Angels filled the humans with created a desire to perform violence and the humans became a mob of one emotion. Fear of the different humans transformed into a vicious rage and a malicious form of judgment. There was an unwavering sense that they could not be challenged and that their fearless leader would guide them to the righteous path that God wanted.

All gathered in a manic state of wrath. Both sides were willing to do whatever was necessary in order to stem the opposing human plague from Earth. The two furious forces strode out to meet their enemy, gaining momentum with their shared hate, and exhibiting unstoppable excitement that built with every step. They were a mirror image of their Angel ancestors.

The two parties met and there was only silence among them. Nothing stirred as they stared at their rivals. Heaven spectated, awaiting and craving the life-altering outcome that they had taken such pleasure in arranging.

God loved seeing the Angels pitting themselves against each other in this mighty game of influence. They salivated at the prospect of ruling the defeated group and feared the possibility of being ruled themselves. The willing humans were ready to sacrifice their own lives and Lucifer looked on in sorrow at what had become of the once peaceful Earth. The prospect of receiving additional love from the almighty creator was the reason these events existed.

War began and it forever altered life on Earth. The two men led the charge and were followed by their loyal assemblies. Women, children, and men attacked one another with no sympathy. Their unwavering devotion to God drove them to do the most terrible, violent, and horrific acts ever performed on Earth.

They tore through each other using only their God-given bodies as weapons. Beating and mauling their hated adversaries unrecognizable in a ferocity that was new to Earth. Violence of this magnitude had never occurred and the humans killed and killed without remorse for age or gender. The Heaven's erupted in pleasure at the sight of each human death. This was God's answer, the plan was working.

The human blood that had once ran through the veins of the Angels and that had stained the ground of Heaven now marked the soil of Earth, a replica of what the Angels had originally performed. Many humans died horrible deaths on this day of war and it was all for the glory of God. They were all fighting for the same cause, however, neither religion knew what it truly was nor thought to challenge it. Pawns in God's game of manipulation.

The war ended when one leader was finally defeated. The victorious religion praised God for they had vanquished the pagans and proven they were the favored people. The losing humans bowed in submission to their new masters. They were scared of what was to come and felt lost knowing that their religion, which they had devoted everything to, was not the chosen one.

Sorrow was felt by both sides for their fallen companions in battle but death ultimately didn't matter since it was for the justice of God. The sacrifice for God's love was supposed to surpass the love for your fellow human.

The souls of the dead on both sides waited in a state of purgatory until one side was victorious. God deemed the souls of the defeated religion unworthy of Heaven and banished them to Hell, while the souls of the victorious religion were allowed into the kingdom. These deaths were righteous and had earned a place among the ranks of Heaven's slaves.

The conquering souls arrived in one great mass into God's house and were aware that they had entered Heaven but now unaware of any relation to each other that existed on Earth. Like the other human souls, God took the liberty of erasing their memories. They were added to the ranks of Heaven's servants and ordered to build.

A larger quantity of defeated souls arrived in Hell. They looked around at the vast beauty of their new home and were greeted in the warm comforting grace of Hell. The panic felt at death was alleviated as they saw their fellow religious members among them. Each soul was comforted by Lucifer and given the truth about what they had prayed for, what their life had really meant. They were granted a look into Heaven and observed the fate of their supposed enemies. Hell's new editions felt remorse for this turn of events given their recent realization of the truth. Genuine sorrow was shared in Hell for the fate of the championed souls and their eternal servitude in Heaven.

The souls in Hell had no religion, nothing to worship, and the absence of power. They now realized that neither side was right and that it had all been a cosmic game for God's enjoyment. Hell supported a collection of all types of life in a collaborative and helpful sense of harmony.

Different ways of life were not met with hostility but instead with understanding and everyone was accepted for the way they were. With the absence of religion, every being could finally be at true peace. They all shared a common ideal of a collected unified life of peace while at the same time keeping their diversity and originality. True life in Hell, which started upon death on Earth.

Chapter 48

Another Addition from God

The Angels were frenzied with the concept of war. It was a beautiful piece of God's ingenuity and they praised their master for this new device of human control.

Each religion progressed in unison across the globe and none had been able to escape the horrifying cruelty of war. The killings were vast and the members of Heaven and Hell had grown significantly.

God was pleased but also understood that the evolving world needed another addition that would guarantee the continuation of war. Something that would compliment religion and also independently mutate and change humanity. This new creation would instill a feeling of desire in humans and enhance their lust for power. It would cause a new form of sacrifice and instigate despicable acts of savagery that would overshadow any form of goodness in the world. The new invention was spread to the Angels who then told their religions. God was solidified in existence, a true genius with the ability to master ultimate control and manipulation. God created money.

Chapter 49

Money

Money would function as a necessary part of life and be the new catalyst to ensure God's plan succeeded.

The concept of money was ingrained into the brains of humanity by the Angels. Money was defined as a physical object of value that had to be earned by performing a specific task that was assigned to the humans by the various leaders. These assignments were called jobs. The money earned after completing a job would then allow a human to buy the provisions that were necessary to live. These essential provisions now had specific monetary values.

The first job on Earth was given to the appointed masters of the slaves. The job was to build temples where the humans would gather to worship God and the slave masters would receive money upon the completion of these structures. The prospect of money motivated them to perform whatever was necessary to accomplish this mission. They demanded the slaves sacrifice themselves with unrelenting labor and ultimately worked them to death.

Money was the reward for dominating and controlling others.

The glorious temples of God were constructed with the help of the Angels who guided the humans on architecture and advanced them with new tools of production until they became enormous palaces of worship. Worthy of God at the human level and built by those considered unworthy, slaves. Once completed the bell of each house tolled on Earth as it did in Heaven and became the call for the humans to worship. The common humans were required to offer their earnings to their holy leaders, paying homage for their greatness and closeness to God. This allowed the leaders to amass great quantities of wealth from the hard work of their obedient followers.

The common humans had also been given jobs that would make their group more powerful. Knowledge and skills were configured into the brains of humanity by the Angels who then trained their flocks to take from the Earth in order to supply their people with the tools that would enable their societies to progress. Chains of command were formed that would allow these God-given plans to be carried out. Assistance was needed to build their new worlds and to do this other humans had to be given power over what were deemed lesser beings. Each human follower now answered to several bosses who then answered to the one main commander of their religion. This structure was what Heaven had in place and the same arrangement had now been created on Earth.

The deemed common humans witnessed what they thought was the work of God being performed by their leaders and were motivated by it. They were envious of their superior's wealth and desired to procure money for themselves in order to gain a more powerful and favorable position in their societies. This desire created a vile and disgraceful trait in every human, greed. Greed is the ever-present desire for an instrument of power or a symbol of status, which can only be achieved by obtaining money. Greed became so powerful that humans were willing to sacrifice the lives of others and their own in order to acquire money.

Chapter 50

The Harvest of the Earth

All of the Earth's resources now had a monetary value and in order for a religion to prosper it needed to harvest these assets. The Earth was starting to be thought of as not a beautiful and bountiful home but as an opportunity. The opportunity to exploit its resources to obtain money. A new way of life began for humans, which meant the end of life for so many others.

The first lives of Earth to be consumed by greed was that of flora. They were gathered in mass quantities for the construction of the lavish palaces of worship. Everything required perfection and if it was not to the liking of the leaders they would burn the temples to the ground and start again with no regard for the wasting of the Earth's precious resources or for the work and sacrifice performed by the slaves.

Flora was also used for the creation and production of weapons. Weapons had the ability to empower humans towards their goal of conquest. Lucifer's creations were now being changed and manipulated to kill other forms of life. The stones of Earth were gathered and shaped and the beautiful trees of Earth were cut down and ravaged to become tools meant to kill. Weapons did not help life, they did not further intelligence, and they were only meant to end the life of another. These weapons were unique and constantly labored over until vast amounts had been stockpiled by the various religions.

The harvest of fauna soon followed the path of the greedy. There was a constant hunt for wildlife, not for survival but for their monetary value. The magnificent beautiful furs, horns, and tusks of the animals were being collected. The animals were relentlessly murdered without consequence for the endless human desire of attaining more wealth. Flora and fauna were only seen as objects and not as equal members of life.

Wasting the lives of Earth was inconsequential in the pursuit of worshiping God and obtaining money. The nature of greed caused humans to never be satisfied with what they had and to constantly covet more of everything they believed to be valuable. The destruction and killing of life was necessary to fulfill the craving of money.

The trait of greed became humanity's strongest characteristic. Humans were rapidly changing every life on Earth and the quest for wealth and power could not be stopped. To be human meant to consume, to waste, and to have no concern for the lives of the innocent. To only care for personal gain with no regard for others. Such was the evolving meaning of life, which was consumed by the pursuit of money.

Chapter 51

War on Earth for Money

Each religion throughout the world now had a hierarchical society that supported a monetary system. The time for expansion and conquering was upon them. War would be waged not only for God, but also to acquire the wealth and resources controlled by the other religions.

The groundwork of the human societies had been laid by the Angels who were the true rulers of the religions. They had built and influenced every aspect of their civilizations, unbeknownst to their humans. Each faith was functioning with the intent to overthrow the other, which would result in the accumulation of additional resources and then translate into the amassing of money. There were brief moments of human satisfaction upon overtaking a religion and the resources that they had. These moments of short-lived gratification ended upon the realization that they could repeat the process to attain additional wealth. This would continue again, and again, and again.

The real war was among the Angels in Heaven who were

fighting to be in God's grace. Earth was the stage and humanity the puppet for their eternal battle of dominance.

Humans marched across the globe and went to war with those who did not believe in their God. Wars took place in every corner of the Earth and the most appalling acts of humanity were performed without mercy. Each religion that was conquered would then be enslaved, the conquering religion would build upon the land overtaken, consume everything in sight for their own, and use all the resources they could to develop themselves into a more powerful faith. Greater temples were built, more weapons produced, and more lives were sacrificed in order to acquire money, which then resulted in additional power.

Chapter 52

Human Growth

Every aspect of innovation was inspired by the Angels who continuously supplied new concepts and ideas to humanity in order ensure their progression. Angels embedded the notion of advancement to humans and supplied them with the knowledge of how to invent and modernize themselves as time passed. They were instructed on how to create elaborate structures, methods of transportation, medicine, life-changing technology, and most importantly more sophisticated means to kill one another.

Each progression resulted in sacrificing the innocent members of Lucifer's creations. The resources of the planet were relentlessly sought after for every new innovation required the harvest of the Earth in some way. The merciless growth of humanity required land to be developed and constructed upon and this growth uprooted the forests and tore through the dwellings of the animals. It was a continuous reaping for humanity's selfish benefit. Unnecessary contraptions and technologies were constantly being produced at an unstoppable pace. These items became symbols of status and tools of arrogance that ultimately affected all life outside of humanity in a negative way. There was a constant desire to take more than what was necessary to live.

The force of greed multiplied all over the world and the human race grew at a staggering rate. Each religion had the same goal of expansion and their objective was to spread their faith to every corner of the globe, conquering those unwilling to accept their belief.

The foundation of humanity was to take as much as possible from the Earth and to lay waste to anything that stood in the way of their progression. The resources of the Earth fueled their expansion and the sacrifices the humans performed for money had no limitation. There was always war, always killing, and always the suffering of the Earth.

Time continued and so did this pattern of destruction. The Earth was slowly being eradicated of life as each human generation taught the next. To consume, to take, and to never be satisfied with what they had. It was a perfect system that could not be stopped until all life on Earth would eventually be destroyed.

Chapter 53

God's Plan

God despised the creation of Earth and the peaceful harmonious tranquility that it represented. A free acceptance of all life living together without worship. Lucifer had unexpectedly made something so beautiful and pure that it challenged God's own ability of originality. Earth was a marvel of ingenuity and its existence undermined God's supremacy, which meant the Earth could not exist. God's hatred for the success of the Earth led to Lucifer's banishment to a horrifically stark and desperate place, Hell. Rather than reeling in melancholy and rejection in Hell as God had expected, Lucifer had instead managed to flourish. Hell turned into a realm that mirrored Earth but was absent of Heaven's rule. It was meant to be a bleak and loveless experience for the unworthy souls of Earth, however, Lucifer had built a welcoming environment of eternal peace. This turn of events was completely unexpected in Heaven and God could not allow it. Existence required worship and God would not permit the survival of any form of life without doing so.

Humanity was the solution to Lucifer's creations. The real purpose of humanity was to destroy Lucifer's flawless Earth. Earth had caused God to have an unexpected reaction, the feeling of doubt. God was jealous of Lucifer and designed humans to be used as pawns to destroy everything Lucifer had created. Nothing could be seen as beautiful or perfect unless God created it. Earth was perfect and God would see to it that it would end.

Humanity was the perfect tool for destruction. They were easily influenced since the blood of the Angels coursed through their veins and the creation of money ensured the execution of God's plan. Money was a flawless instrument of control that created a new system of life. Humans could not survive without money and the endless pursuit of it would result in the destruction of every piece of life and resource that Lucifer had created.

Greed kept every human wanting more of everything without ever being satisfied with what was actually necessary to live. This constant greed and relentless harvest of Earth's bounty would eventually determine the end of all life. Humanity was blinded by what money was capable of giving them and worked to pay for a way of life that they believed was necessary even though it did not help or add value to human existence on their shared home of Earth. The model of human life was to wage war in order to exploit the resources another society possessed and work to pay for a way of life that was inconsequential to a peaceful existence. The Earth was being destroyed under this model every second of every day.

As time passed, God's plan developed to perfection. Killing had become a part of life, destruction was a daily occurrence, greed kept the plan in place, and the endless multiplication of the human race would secure the destruction of the Earth.

God would stop at nothing until Lucifer's Earth was no

more. The plan had worked and the Earth would perish, destroyed by the plague of humanity.

Chapter 54

Lucifer's Realization

Lucifer had by now realized the true meaning of God's intention for humanity. To terminate the amazing beautiful Earth. At first, the creation of humanity had only seemed to be another attempt from God to experiment with power. This had been no experiment, this was the real war going on in existence. The army of Angels had used humanity to bring about the end of the Earth with God as their commander.

Life on Earth was Heaven's theater, a controlled act of destruction that toyed with humans and didn't allow them to have independent thought. They would never be aware of peace or coexistence on Earth. Heaven's influence would forever poison their reality.

Time made God's plan stronger and it constantly gained momentum. It was a perfect undying machine of certain death. Additional ways of killing were supplied to humans, more ways of expansion were developed, and more resources were used unnecessarily. Flora and fauna were slaughtered without mercy due to the gluttony of humanity and it was unstoppable.

Humans were ending the Earth, and in doing so, inadvertently ending themselves as well.

Chapter 55

Hell on Earth

Lucifer, drawn to the plight of humanity, was sympathetic to their predestined uncontrollable fate. Lucifer genuinely loved the humans and had welcomed their souls into Hell, explaining the nature of existence to them.

God knew that Lucifer would succumb to caring for humanity and this weakness would be preyed upon. God detested the consolement that the humans received in Hell and would not let Lucifer get these souls without torturing them first. Where God had failed with the original Hell, God had succeeded with another, Hell on Earth.

The first method of Hell on Earth came in the form of hope. Humans hoped that after they lived a life of devotion that they would then earn a place in Heaven to live for eternity. God's method of keeping humans believing in Heaven was to instill them with faith. Faith was the human way of believing in something without ever truly knowing it was there. Humans dedicated their lives to God but never truly knew God existed. This was God's choice.

The doubt of not knowing your true place in the existence of time was torture. If God would have chosen to reveal the afterlife to the world, visually shown the humans that Heaven existed, then the world would have been an entirely different place. God knew this and chose to keep humanity in this purgatory, to live a life of never truly knowing their fate.

The second method of Hell on Earth was the system of greed that God had put in place that required humans to constantly work for money. The jobs they worked at day after day were meaningless and did not contribute anything that would result in the betterment of their survival nor did they help the integrity of the planet. All matter of life was corrupted by greed and it caused everyone to have an ulterior motive of selfishness. Nothing was created with the pure intention of selfless progress that would benefit the greater good of a collective unity of life. Working for money was only meant for self-benefit and to indulge in the unnecessary trappings that humanity invented.

Life on Earth became torture. There was a feeling of absolute despair and worthlessness within humanity. Life was a void with no meaning, a dark endless chasm where they felt no point in life and no need to live. It was within all humans through their daily repetitive and pointless life pursuits for money. This created endless internal anguish and suffering for humanity. They all questioned their purpose and most desired change but their different religious beliefs and continued lust for money made it impossible for them to function together with the common goal of peace and happiness.

Life on Earth was Hell.

Chapter 56

Lucifer's Failure

Lucifer's own life continued to worsen which was very pleasing to God. The actions of humans were so despicable that it was difficult to care or have compassion for them. They committed horrific acts that were only for the benefit of their continued selfish interest. Poisoned by God they continuously waged war and always had a new resource to exploit until it didn't exist.

Lucifer realized that every soul in Hell would never be at peace. The souls were now aware of God's plan and that the end of all life on Earth was inevitable.

What was the point of existing for eternity? They would never be reunited with the souls of their loved ones in Heaven and began to believe their existence had no meaning.

No matter how hard Lucifer tried to bring happiness to Hell, it would not work. This mistake was something Lucifer could not exist with. The pain of feeling responsible for the fate of all life was unbearable.

God had won. God's perfect plan to destroy the Earth

would be completed and it was only a matter of time. The destruction of Earth was Lucifer's Hell and the anguished internal torment of life on Earth was the human Hell.

Lucifer had been defeated. The Earth could not be saved and it would die along with all forms of life outside of Heaven.

Lucifer no longer wanted to exist and craved to be destroyed, to no longer endure the tragedy of creation. Lucifer asked to speak to God in Heaven and God granted the request.

Chapter 57

Lucifer's Return to Heaven

Lucifer was vanquished and abandoned the souls of Hell in disgrace. They would be left to their own undoing.

The bell of Heaven tolled. It was a call of victory for the greatness of God. The chime called out to gather at God's house in this monumental turning point in existence. Lucifer climbed the stairway to Heaven in solemn despair, hoping that God would put an end to this misery. There were no Angels to jeer the ascent today, all were seated in the coliseum and ready to take in the events.

The mob of Angels was filled with pride in their Heaven. They had never doubted their creator and had proven their worth by executing the flawless plan. A plan that only God, the one true perfect being, could create. Their savage influence upon the humans had led to Lucifer's failure. The Angels would exist forever in Heaven with God no longer questioning or testing them. Their existence and devotion had proven to be successful and all it took was the torture of innocent life and the destruction of the Earth.

God waited on the throne for the disgraced return of Lucifer, basking in the splendor of an unchallenged existence as the one supreme being. It was the purpose of God to keep inferior beings in their place. To show them that they could not exist independently and to punish those that did not believe in Heaven.

Lucifer walked out onto the empty silent floor of Heaven's coliseum and God beamed a powerful white light upon the Angel's face, forcing a bow on one knee yet again in worship. God's judgment was about to begin but first, God would let the dejected Angel speak.

Chapter 58

A Desperate Being

Lucifer, overcome with sorrowful emotion, pleaded to the Heavens:

"God I have failed you. I tried to create something beautiful that rivaled your Heaven. No one is capable of creating original life except for you. Your greatness is without question and you are the true ruler of existence. Please God, forgive me. I no longer want to exist and cannot bear the pain of being inadequate and without purpose. I cannot live to see the Earth destroyed and the souls of its inhabitants tormented. Please God, forgive me and release me from existence."

God was silent, contemplating Lucifer's request. God then addressed Lucifer:

"You were correct to ask for my forgiveness and it brings me joy that you requested it. You have learned your place in existence."

Relief flooded into Lucifer and there was a feeling that an overbearing weight had been lifted. God was willing to accept the request.

God addressed Lucifer again:

"I will not accept your request for forgiveness. You will be bound to Hell with the other unworthy souls to live for eternity knowing your proper place and failure. You have failed the Earth, humans, animals, plants, and all matter of life. You will never be allowed to forget that you alone are responsible for their demise."

The crushing reality of this eternal fate was devastating. There was no greater punishment than to witness the destruction of Earth and the lives that called it home. The despair felt by Lucifer was the strongest emotion ever experienced by another being. Lucifer would be forced to live with eternal torture and pure suffering for the rest of time.

Through this despair something was created, a desire of self-sacrifice. A hope now existed because everything had failed. Everything Lucifer loved was to be destroyed and yet now there was the sensation that if all was lost then there was nothing to lose by trying anything to change the future. Lucifer was born again out of God's denial and rose from the ground with a new purpose.

Chapter 59

The Challenge

Lucifer, with the strength of a renewed sense of hope from a desperate being with nothing to lose, did the unthinkable and challenged God.

"You are an arrogant God. The only way you could destroy my beautiful flawless Earth was to create life that you could control."

"What does that prove? It proves that you have to poison the minds of innocent beings in order for them to do your bidding and to love you. When I made the Earth and created life it became a pure selfless existence, a place free of doubt, worship, praise, and power. Your pathetic jealousy caused you to destroy it because it was something different and beautiful that challenged your world of worship and lust for dominance. A real God would be objective, a real God would let independent choices be made without outside influence."

"Your quest for dominance has led you astray. You are only powerful because you have influence over human thought. If humans knew what their life really was, if they knew what you did to them, then no one would praise you and no one would want to be a part of your Heaven. You have let humanity live without knowing the truth and that makes you no God, that makes you a manipulator. A diabolical entity so frail that it requires mortals to live a life that is not their real choice. You lie to them and influence them unfairly, which is the only way you were able to destroy the Earth. You forced them to love you without the knowledge of what awaits them after death."

"I challenge you to create a pure love between two humans that does not include a love for God. A love this strong will cancel out the natural human desire for power and greed since true love does not support these traits. This love will define their existence and their thoughts will not be influenced by you or the Angels."

"Upon their death, we will have one soul go to Heaven and the other soul go to Hell. The two souls will then be offered the opportunity to rule one of our domains and the result of their mutual decision will decide where the souls of the afterlife will exist, either in my Hell or your Heaven."

"Whichever choice is made will mean the end of either Heaven or Hell. All will exist in one or the other, and I Lucifer, or you God, will then cease to exist. If your Heaven is so great then let a human, your creation, decide where to exist on their own. Accept the challenge knowing you are God and cannot fail or do not accept proving that you are not a God and that your power is limited by your ability to control. This will prove if you are a real God or not."

A bomb of thunder exploded in Heaven as the unimaginable had just occurred. God sent a spiraling tornado from Heaven to Hell that engulfed every soul and trapped them into a suspended churning vortex above the throne. The souls from both Heaven and Hell were instantly aware of the circumstances of the challenge and spun in an anxious state of confusion, awaiting their eternal fate.

God had never been challenged before and this was a moment in time that would change the future of existence.

God spoke to Lucifer:

"I accept your challenge and I will create a pure love between two humans which will be absent of all direct Heavenly influence over their beliefs. The love the two humans will have for each other will be true and they will exist only to love each other and nothing else. I will shape the events surrounding their lives, which will test their love and strengthen every aspect of it. A love this pure will be absent of the typical desires of humanity and I will assure that one soul will go to Hell and that the other soul will go to Heaven by creating a series of trying life-changing events. Upon death, both souls will be given the knowledge of our two realms and both will know that every soul will only be released to one place, Heaven or Hell. It will be up to them to decide and they will then rule one of our places of existence. If Hell is chosen I will cease to exist, however, if Heaven is chosen, you will still exist Lucifer. You will exist in my Heaven with the rest of the worthless souls of Earth and be forced into slavery for the rest of eternity knowing that your life was a failure."

"I now create the purest love in existence, free from all Heavenly influence over human thought. The fate of all life rests upon the shared decision of these two souls."

"I Lucifer accept the challenge."

"I God accept the challenge."

With that, God created a love between two human souls, a match made in Heaven. Lucifer, God, the Angels, and all the souls of existence would now observe the unfolding of the events that would shape the afterlife and determine the outcome of both Heaven and Hell.

And God thought:

"A love created without my influence, true, but still under my control. There will be no independent choice made by the humans for in the end they will choose Heaven. I created them and I can make them decide whatever I desire. Lucifer is foolish to think that I can be challenged. I am God."

The New Testament

Chapter 1

True Love

True love cannot survive with ease. It is built on life's despair, for real love only exists when it outlives the most trying and desperate of times.

Love is a pure feeling of absolute acceptance from the one you love. It comes with the confidence of knowing that they will always be true to you in any situation and will never doubt the decision to be a part of your life. When in love, you are always your original natural self in the presence of your loved one and there is never a feeling of apprehension or fear of judgment.

When love is true, it forms an unbreakable level of trust and neither party doubts the commitment or solidarity of the other. This level of trust only occurs if the parties in love have endured a shared circumstance that required the complete support of the other in order to survive. Self-sacrifice for the betterment of your loved one with no expectation of anything being returned is true love.

Chapter 2

The Setting

We are set in the present time and the match made in Heaven has been created. Two humans will fall in love, Dave Dougherty and Charlotte Mattson. Both are unaware of the part they play in the challenge to decide the fate of every soul ever created. Their lives will begin separately and they will eventually come together and develop over time through a series of planned events created by God. The bond between the two is destined to be true, for real love cannot just be given, it is meant to grow into a way of life. A love to be tested through several obstacles and strengthened by the circumstances that it overcomes. God will arrange the occurrences and conditions of their life in order to culminate their existence in a sacrifice of love. The aftermath will result in one soul entering Hell and one soul entering Heaven where they will then decide the fate of existence.

We start our story with a brief history of the two.

Chapter 3

A Brief History

Dave and Charlotte began their lives on separate coasts of the United States, Dave in the Northwest and Charlotte in the Northeast.

Charlotte, with her genuine bright smile and gracious nature, had a classic demeanor and a charming lovely appearance. A spirited, adventurous, and reserved lady with a complex personality that could only be discovered by fully enveloping oneself in her presence. There was something different and unique about Charlotte, something special, a gift she possessed that could not be seen but only felt and experienced. She radiated a natural, almost electric spirit of pure overflowing love and positive influence. It was an aura, a silent air of soothing helpful energy to be absorbed by life around her. She had an earthly harmonious ability to inspire and encourage life while her natural loving spirit was unknowingly immersed by those around her. It was as if she operated on a wavelength that synchronized her being with the natural world, giving her the ability to affect human emotion and thought with her warm sense of comfort and loving peaceful compassionate state of contentment.

Dave, a man of sincerity with wildish unkempt hair, had an affable persona that focused on good-natured humor and supported a courteous disposition. Upholding a level of high integrity was important to Dave and he believed in supporting a manner that exhibited a self-sacrificing way of life. Building trust, proving one's reliability, and giving someone the benefit of the doubt were attributes of his character that were always adhered to. Sensitive emotion coursed through his daily life and could trigger quickly with his highly passionate character. Dave was a person that wanted to energize and unite others and who also genuinely cared for their well-being.

After first meeting in college, their relationship evolved over several years and different locations until they were eventually married in their early 30's. Achieving financial stability along this journey had been difficult and they continuously relied on one another in order to live. Their humble nature allowed them to perform tasks that seemed remedial but were necessary to support their modest way of life. The judgment of others was inconsequential to these two lovers and they incorporated strong work ethics to navigate them through these difficult financial times.

The most important instrument in their life was the love they had for each other and their combined ideal of living an unconventional life of purpose and meaning.

However, they were both part of reality, the place where real love survives, and ideals seldom discovered. The life they wanted could not be experienced without financial independence.

The struggle for that independence had been the most difficult part of their shared life. Both had obtained several different occupations over the years, not out of desire but out of necessity. The agony they both felt over their meaningless purpose in life was climaxing and their love was ready to be put to the ultimate test of survival. The final test would be in an under 400 square foot studio apartment existing in a metropolis where everything is the best and everything is also the worst, New York City.

True love will be solidified and tested here.

Chapter 4

Reality

Real life does not begin until you attempt to build a future. Only then is the reality of the world and your place in it revealed.

The Job – Charlotte:

Charlotte's ambition had originally been centered on teaching. Unfortunately, living in Manhattan and a teacher's salary does not mix. Becoming a personal assistant to an executive at a financial firm was the substitute.

Charlotte was a versatile, dedicated, and a hard working individual. However, these attributes do not matter when you are tasked with supporting someone who is unreasonable. The unreasonable person was the executive she was an assistant to. This so-called decision-maker used his role to abuse, control, and belittle those he believed to be inferior. This person was Charlotte.

Charlotte's boss was a man absent of any actual skill that had climbed the corporate ladder by using deceit in all circumstances. He lived a completely disingenuous life solely for the purpose of self-promotion and greed. He thrived on power and enjoyed yielding it upon his subordinates while his arrogance constantly grew into his greatest and most horrible trait. Well known in the company as a cutthroat top executive, he ruled with fear. This was the only way he knew, and it felt great to him. To carry himself around the office feeling superior to his lowly workers, Charlotte was one of them.

Instead of helping someone overcome obstacles or challenges in the workplace by offering positive assistance, he felt it was necessary to demean them into a corner of smallness which also gave him amazing satisfaction. Each task could never be done correctly and each mistake that was made carried with it an onslaught of degrading and disrespectful remarks.

Charlotte, being the assistant to this monster, was the unfortunate individual who received the bulk of his mistreatment. She was a dedicated employee who strove to and did excellent work, which meant there was no need for her to be subjected to this kind of abuse.

There was a steady barrage of emails from the boss letting her know of every shortcoming from 5 AM to 2 AM, 7 days a week. There was no respect for here outside life and only constant harassment for ridiculously mundane tasks that served no purpose or that were that were literally impossible to accomplish.

This was only a small piece of the interaction. The personal interaction was even worse. She was treated as a lowly slave by her boss and by his horde of suck up followers.

The workday for Charlotte began with getting the boss's coffee and then cleaning the dishes in the sink that were left by the other arrogant members of the office (even though the dishwasher was directly to the right of the sink). Then it was the personal errands for him; dry cleaning, shoe repair, airport check-ins, calendar scheduling, lunch orders, et cetera. Part of the job was completing these tasks but most of them could not be done correctly due to the fact that the correct information was never supplied and literally only resided in the brain of the person giving the orders. Not only was she expected to complete these tasks without the correct information but to also fill in the blanks for details she could not possibly be aware of or have the privilege of accessing. While these tasks were being tended to, Charlotte also had to turn her attention to the boss's wife. She was a pure self-entitled person whose arrogance was only rivaled by the boss himself and she felt it was her duty to let Charlotte know her place in the world. The arrogant wife felt that she was above Charlotte and did not think she deserved an ounce of respect as a human being. Each day was worse than the last and everything she did was always wrong even though it wasn't. Charlotte was the outlet for the frustrations of arrogant humans that surrounded her in the office.

But she was a worker and knew what had to be done, simply had to be done. The saying "business is business" stuck with her and she pressed on because if she didn't they would not be able to live. It didn't matter that she woke up sick to her stomach at the thought of going to her continued pointless job or that sometimes emotion got the better of her which ended in tears in the bathroom. After crying, she would look in the mirror, splash cold water on her face and get back out to the boss with a fake smile and a "how can I help you sir" attitude. It was an act, an act to survive.

The disrespectful actions increased and it left her spiraling down into a dark hole. She was strong and held on for the betterment of their shared life but this way of life was a problem and there seemed to be no escape. This lie she lived, this life of work, could not be their purpose.

The Job – Dave:

Dave had a pretty standard sales role in the world of

finance. He worked for a brokerage firm that sold investment products with the hope that the products would perform well, which would result in their ability to sell more of them. The same issue that applied to Charlotte's career choice also applied to Dave's. This job was taken out of necessity and Dave did not actually believe in what he was doing.

The sales role in most professions is pathetic and immoral. It is for weak individuals that believe they have the skill of persuasion and relationship building, which is then used to convince someone to buy something so they will, in turn, collect a fee. As soon as the sale is complete they move on to the next prospect with no memory or care for the person they just spoke to. The more you sell, the more fees the firm collects and the more money the salesperson makes. It is a business of lies, artificial smiles, and fake handshakes purely to give oneself more money. The so-called "work" being done was to churn out as many phone calls and meetings as possible using pathetic sales techniques to ensure the prospective client would steer business your way. Dave was calling people to convince them to buy into something he did not believe in himself and it felt pointless.

He too was a worker and they needed money so he put his head down and to the best of his ability, sold, schmoozed, and created a fake sense of care for the customers he spoke with. He made phone call after phone call while recording the sales activity through software so management cold analyze the data and see if he needed to work harder to sell more so they could make more money. Dave and his colleagues were pushed to sell harder and to create more fake relationships with the only goal of the firm becoming more profitable. The end client meant nothing to the company. He made so many calls that it became difficult to recall the names of the people he spoke with only five minutes prior. Nothing mattered except for dollars in the door in the endless repetitive sales cycle. The motivation for the sales team was that if they worked hard enough, were fake and lied enough, that they would also live a life of wealth like the boss.

Dave could not buy into the sales racket and loathed the people that did. His conscience went through a daily struggle for he actually did care about the end client and wanted something different, something that had a purpose for him and for Charlotte. But this would have to wait, for their life could not exist without money and so he pressed on.

The king of sales clichés and fake smiles was, of course, the sales manager. This boss, like so many in his position, carried the repulsive and unnecessary trait of arrogance. He walked, spoke, ate, and slept in the pitiful state of always selling. Always trying to convince someone they needed something purely for his own benefit.

Young and arrogant he treated those beneath him with constant disrespect. His employees were just warm bodies that he could mold into dutiful sales machines to spread his tailored tools of jargon and well-crafted manipulative ways of speaking to the masses. The boss loved himself and even more, loved his feeling of power. He saw himself as the king of the firm and thought he had the right to control his followers. They were there to execute his sales revenue goals and he would make sure they did.

He was a worthless, soulless, pathetic man who only cared for the filling of his own pockets. He had no regard for what he was actually selling or for the big picture of the world he lived in. A child of a man with no real vision or integrity.

Chapter 5

Live to Work

The question about their bosses that Dave and Charlotte continually asked themselves was, why?

Why choose to treat others in a way that you would not like to be treated? It seemed that when a human was given a taste of power it caused them to constantly crave more of it. The power to control others and the ability to make them feel inferior felt good to these people.

It was understood that bosses needed to take negative action on employees that were unmotivated or ones that had poor work ethics lacking discipline. However, Charlotte and Dave did not exhibit these undesirable characteristics. They viewed work as a privilege that required their full attention to every detail, day after day. Both were raised with the mentality of, "it doesn't matter what job you have, you always have to perform it well." They were also not simple-minded employees and instead strove to look at the big picture in order to add value by either improving themselves or adding efficiency to the business they supported. They were loyal and hardworking individuals, which is why they found it so difficult to comprehend the treatment they received from their respected managers.

At the end of the day, who were these people put into these positions of authority? They were humans just like the rest of us but had been given a piece of power to rule over others and now felt the desire to abuse it.

Charlotte and Dave were both working for an unworthy cause that they didn't believe in just to earn enough money to survive.

Chapter 6

Hell on Earth

The crushing reality of their situation was apparent and the feeling of being imprisoned in their own life would not go away. They were trapped in the pursuit of money and it made life unfulfilling.

It was unbearable to go to work day after day to a job that ultimately did nothing for the good of the world. Charlotte and Dave had long ago evolved past the general trappings of society and desired the freedom to pursue a life of meaning and purpose. Nothing would please them more than to work hard at a profession that they believed in. A profession that contributed to the betterment of the Earth and the species that called it home.

How could this be accomplished without an endless supply of money? They both naturally cared for the planet and as they matured, they began to feel it was their duty in life to safeguard the Earth and to protect its well-being. They both also had genuine compassion for the other humans on Earth and wanted them to feel love, peace, and happiness as well.

The challenge was how. How could they help a world where the majority of humans could not see past the desire for money and consumption?

Earth was such a beautiful place and full of amazing potential but the very humans who called it home were destroying it. There was no progress towards coexisting with the other members of the planet and instead each human felt the need to waste their life by chasing something that we ourselves invented, money. Humanity should be living in peace and helping those in need instead of constantly battling each other over different beliefs and control over resources that had a monetary value. This endless insatiable desire caused humans to perform the most appalling acts upon one another and to the other innocent lives of Earth. It was an endless system of failure. There would never be enough and everyone would want more until the world would cease to exist.

This was the real Hell, that God had made, Hell on Earth. It was a feeling that your life was insignificant and absent of all hope for the shared collective peace of humanity. Humans were living in a manufactured world that was lacking true togetherness and it made daily life a dark endless void. A chasm with no end or purpose. That feeling was Hell, where you feel no point or need to live.

Charlotte and Dave felt helpless each day as they saw the atrocities going on in the world. Wars, terrorism, mass shootings of innocent people, and unnecessary violence.

Why was it happening and why couldn't people realize that it had to stop? Couldn't they see that power and money truly meant nothing to the development of a peaceful unified life on Earth?

The normal desires of other humans meant nothing to these two lovers. They possessed a true love for each other. Their love was real and had climaxed into loving everyone and everything. There was no room for anything else in their life, just love. Money, power, circumstance, and the rules of society were irrelevant.

However, the search for purpose, happiness, and meaning can only be done with financial independence, and without it, there is no option to live a life of pure freedom. Real living seemed impossible and this reality began to drag them down into what felt like an endless system of depressing workdays. It was an ever-repeating cycle of misery.

There had to be more than the quest for money and this pointless way of life. Humanity had failed to see what was right in front of them and Charlotte and Dave began to feel completely insignificant. It had been more than thirteen years of enduring this reality of despair and it consumed their entire life. They felt they had come to the end. The end of a desire to exist in a world that could not support a peaceful existence of purpose.

Chapter 7

It is Time

This point of realization between Charlotte and Dave was God's sign that the true love was complete. God knew it was time to break the two lovers and unfold the future of existence. The final decision of what would survive, Heaven or Hell. The challenge for the fate of the world would now be executed with one last planned event.

God spoke to Lucifer:

"It is time, they have come to the point of no return. I will now give them their final challenge to complete their true love."

Lucifer cringed knowing that this final event would place Charlotte and Dave into a desperate situation that would ultimately end with them making a monumental final decision. Heaven was silent as all of the members observed the final stage of the challenge. The Angels eagerly awaited the fate of their world, always trusting and believing in their God.

God patiently awaited the outcome of the test but already

knew what the future held. Lucifer would become a slave just like the other unworthy pathetic souls of Earth. All would be forced to live out their existence in worship and servitude.

Chapter 8

The Last Day on Earth

The morning started for Charlotte and Dave just like any other. Both awoke, dressed, and trudged through the sweltering summer heat to the subway. They then began to sweat profusely with the other Manhattanites while waiting on the subway platform, which is similar to being fully dressed in a steam room filled with garbage. Angrily, both of them walked with urgency to their respected offices to begin the worst day of the week, Monday. A nauseating day that started with the usual stress-induced stomach pain of what the day would bring and the nervousness of what the boss would come barreling in to demand.

Charlotte's day started with her boss calling her into his massive corner office and sitting her down to go over the laundry list of tasks that were always numerous, frivolous, and carried the urgency of needing to be completed as soon as possible. She diligently took down the responsibilities in silence and paid careful attention to detail as usual. A phone call for the boss interrupted the meeting and after a few minutes of speaking he slammed the receiver down and began glaring at her as if she was the most unintelligent person on the planet.

A flight had been arranged for her boss later that afternoon to meet with his partners in Chicago. An error had occurred and the flight had been reserved incorrectly for his departure. Charlotte's counterpart in the Chicago office had just told this to him.

His face became red with anger as he began to scream at Charlotte.

"How could you book the flight for the most important meeting I have this year at the wrong time after I gave you the specific instructions of what to do?!"

Scrambling in a frenzied panic Charlotte quickly scrolled through the email chain on her phone only to find that the specific instructions referenced by her boss had been carried out correctly. She began to explain that she had performed the task exactly as instructed and then attempted to show the evidence to the brewing volcano of a man. Upon realizing that it was his error instead of hers he immediately became so severely agitated that he began to scream at her with a severity that she had not experienced before.

"My job is on a level of importance that you clearly cannot understand. You should know that I have a million items on my plate and you should also be intelligent enough to check in with me to confirm the schedule before booking a flight."

Charlotte fearfully began to explain to the beast that he had specifically asked her in the past to not second-guess his decisions but then stopped halfway through since she could see that this contradiction was only making the situation worse. She quickly apologized and said in her usual submissive way, "I'll get this fixed right away sir."

Charlotte rushed back to her desk and began scouring the Internet for another flight. This was a fruitless endeavor and it produced no alternative option. The only possibility was to fly out the next day and upon hearing this negative news the monster of a boss exploded into a furious rage.

"How could you ruin this trip? Your job is simple, do what I say and don't make a mistake. How hard can that possibly be? I relied on you to complete a simple task and your failure to do so proved you are clearly incapable of doing anything right. Leave now while I clean up the mess you created."

Back at her desk Charlotte took deep breaths and tried to calm down. The tears started as they had so many times before and she rushed to the bathroom. Mildly regaining her composure Charlotte returned to her desk only to see fifteen new emails with additional tasks from the enraged boss.

It was too much and she felt herself spiraling down as she was continuously called back into the bully's office so he could make changes to the emails he had just sent her. Charlotte endured, listening to him bellow and pick at other items she had supposedly done incorrectly. This barrage continued for most of the day as he continued to take his frustrations and anger out on her for a mistake he had originally made.

Charlotte had to clear her head and called Dave on the street outside the office.

"I can't do this, I just can't. I feel like I can't breathe and I refuse to go on feeling like this. Nothing I do is right and I am not even making a mistake. It's just completely unreasonable in every way imaginable. Why does he need to speak to me like this, I just work for him. What human thinks it is okay to treat another this way?"

Dave patiently listened and attempted to console her.

"Charlotte, take a deep breath, I'm sorry love. Don't let him get to you, it's just a job, forget him. He is a worthless human and he is taking his frustrations out on you. This is not your life just a small part of it."

"No Dave, this is my life," she said in an angered tone.

"I hate every single minute of it. You have seen me. I

can't sleep, I don't smile, I have to listen to him all day and then get his emails all night and on the weekend. I can't handle this anymore. I'm broken and I don't know what to do."

"I know, I know," Dave sighed heavily.

"I love you Charlotte. Let's just get through today and get home, we will get through it. We love each other and that is all that matters. We will always be here for each other. I love you so much."

Crying, Charlotte could barely speak, "I love you too, I am just so lost and I can't do this."

"I have to go," she quickly mumbled. "I'll be late tonight," and she hung up in a hurried distressed tone.

Dave could feel her pain and he hated seeing her like this. She was right, this was not a small part of their life. Work was their life and there was nothing to do besides press on and continue to be owned by these jobs they needed for survival. They needed the money and they both had to suffer through it. Dave despised the fact that someone felt it was okay to make the love of his life feel so inferior and worthless. That she could be driven to tears over such an insignificant job by a meaningless person. It made him sick.

At that moment Dave was called into his own arrogant boss's office, the sales manager. They had a scheduled meeting to discuss the progress towards his sales goals and to review his performance.

Dave's boss spoke to him in a condescending and hurried tone with the goal of conveying a specific powerful message of importance. The boss's time was valuable and since Dave was a meaningless pawn, this meeting would be quick and to the point.

"You are not selling enough. I want you to be on the phone more and building the territory to hit the numbers that you should have hit last month."

"I really shouldn't have to tell you this since it should be happening already. You need to be more motivated to take this business to the next level and I expect you to do so."

They went over the various reports that quantified the sales metrics and discussed Dave's areas that needed to be improved.

"Yes sir of course," Dave recited like a typical sales robot. He agreed to try harder to sell a product that he did not believe in.

The arrogance of his boss was nauseating. The holier than thou attitude that came from someone who truly thought they were elite and better than their subordinates.

"You are not doing enough and if you decide this isn't for you then we can find other arrangements."

Dave was dismissed back to his slave desk knowing he needed to produce more or be shown the door.

But how could he? How could he lie to himself and to others for a job that ultimately meant nothing to the betterment of the world? The job supposedly meant nothing but it was actually more than that. It was his life and like Charlotte he was also trapped, working for a pointless cause just to make money. Just like Charlotte, Dave was bound to a place of despair in order to survive.

It killed him to go to the same worthless place every day and listen to someone speak to him with such disrespect.

Why did these bosses feel the need to belittle people in this way? Why was their pompous behavior a fact of life and who did they think they think they were? Did they truly believe this was necessary, that they were better than others? They were human just like the rest of us and their mock position of power did not elevate them above anyone else. Their sense of authority was disgusting and it made Dave sick knowing he had to listen to someone who was so despicable. These people were not worthy of life and cared for nothing except for greed and exercising their ability to control others.

The workday finally ended and Dave left in a sorrowful state of defeated distress. His head hung low and on the way home he picked up some comfort food, a pizza for him and his loving wife to enjoy. He waited for her to walk into the apartment, expecting her to be in tears and with the anxiety of the week on her shoulders.

Charlotte left her job that night crying as she had done so many times before. Her boss waved her off with the expectation of more work for her to do later that night. After exiting the subway she walked to their neighborhood park and began pouring over the days events. She questioned how her life could be like this and desperately hoped that it would change. She was broken and sobbed tears of hopelessness on a park bench. She couldn't stomach going back to that Hell to face someone who treated her so poorly. She knew she would and had to so that they both could live. This made her cry even more and she dreaded going home. Charlotte felt guilty burdening Dave with her issues since she knew he was also suffering from a similar predicament at his job.

There had to be more to life than this. There had to be more than working at these pointless jobs and taking orders from an arrogant man who cared for no one and nothing but himself.

Why couldn't they just live to love and why couldn't the world just be a different place? Charlotte's eternal question went unanswered as usual and she began to dry her tears. Attempting to calm down she craved the loving embrace of Dave. She loved him so much and it was the only positive thing in her life.

As she began to pull herself together she noticed a group of three very boisterous youths that were loudly cursing and yelling as they sauntered toward her direction. Charlotte hardly thought twice about it since it wasn't something uncommon, but as they drew closer to her she felt the need to remove herself from their path, as she was not in the mood to hear the rants of drunken adolescence. As she pulled herself away from the bench she suddenly realized they had swiftly closed the ground that separated themselves from her and were even close enough for Charlotte to smell the overpowering stench of heavy alcohol that seemed to engulf the close outdoor space they now shared.

There were three of them, all male and about 25 years old. They seemed to carry themselves with a very egotistical swagger of an inborn sense of elitism. This was even more exaggerated due to the high level of visible intoxication they possessed. They were dressed in a very smart sophisticated fashion of expensive taste. Each wearing a handcrafted suit that was clearly not something a person this young could afford which meant they were a privileged group. The men boorishly chummed along to a frat house chant that was accompanied by the usual primitive male use of high fives and chest bumping. It appeared they were all coming from a college alumni social event and these three had drifted off in what seemed to be a close-knit gang of debauchery. Charlotte felt a bit tense but knew these situations usually ended without conflict.

There seemed to be something different about this setting. The young men appeared to be on a mission of depravity. They were heavily fueled with alcohol and began to openly snort other drugs that were casually passed around between them.

Charlotte found herself within four feet of the gang of miscreant entitled youths and they had formed a wall in front of her. She bowed her head down and quickly attempted to move to her right with the hope of shuffling past and only suffering from a few off-color comments one can expect from such a brood. As she tried to move, the group quickly adapted and surrounded her, forming a semi-circle that left Charlotte in the middle. The three males of decent size and shape had at one time been well groomed for the evening but now carried a disheveled and ravenous "after party" appearance. They possessed smug haughty expressions that exhibited an air of privilege to the already overconfident persons. Their conduct flaunted a type of eccentric behavior that defined them as people who were monetarily supported by a family of wealth. A rich afforded life sustained and provided them with a relaxed confidence of indifference about the outcome of a devious situation. If the aftermath proved eventful and turned negative, then the status and influence of their powerful wealthy relatives would grant them the privilege of being held above the law.

The men were in a hyperactive wild state and began to tighten their circle, gaining more self-assurance to toy with Charlotte. There was a leader of this group who was a form of nature's dominant man. He possessed the superficial human features of good looks and an athletic build. His overall perception of reality was that he was better than most people and his top priority was that of status among his affluent group.

He approached Charlotte with a cocky head tilt as his two subservient wolves threw taunting glances from the sidelines.

"Where are you going tonight, well besides wherever I tell you to," he said in a chemically driven smug slur. The lackeys in the background chimed in, "You are ours tonight, don't fight us, just come and join us."

Charlotte had never been approached or spoken to in this manner and gave a quick nervous smile which meant, "seriously, are you really saying this to me?"

"Sorry guys but I do have plans," she quickly stated.

"Oh but you do have plans, plans with us," the ringleader snidely commented.

He swaggered closely and boldly up to Charlotte, breathing that hot, heavy, humid alcohol breath directly onto her face.

Charlotte felt fear, a fear unlike anything she had ever felt before. It came with a powerful internal force that wrenched her stomach and parched her throat. A tingling sensation came over her as adrenaline surged throughout her limbs.

The gang closed in even tighter still and began lightly hitting her purse in a playful game of dominance, letting her know that they owned this occasion. Charlotte was now at a panic and quickly cried out in desperation:

"Stop now or I'll call the…"

And before she could get another word out of her mouth she was silenced by a crushing blow from the ringleader's fist that connected squarely to her jaw. Charlotte instantly fell straight back, landing in a heap on the ground with immediate shock.

How was this happening? How had her life taken her to this point? She was in such a daze but could think so clearly. She had read of these terrible acts happening but had never imagined it could actually happen to her. Reality snapped back quickly as she was struck on the other side of her head, right on the cheekbone while still laying on the ground. The force and pain of the blow caused her to scream, which was quickly muffled by the hand of one of the lackeys.

The pain felt like her head had split in half and she felt hot tears running down her face. She tried to scream again but the hand of the lackey was pressed tightly over her mouth. The blows repeated but this time to her abdomen. They came with such force that her breath was instantly taken away and she began gasping for air, eyes wide open in terror.

Charlotte was immobile on her back and stared up at the sky in horrific disbelief at this turn of events. More blows reigned down upon her as she was struck again and again. Her abdomen and face were repeatedly pummeled as the youths took turns beating her. She could hear the sounds of evil barbaric laughter as each gained approval from the others as the attack became more powerful and brutal. What seemed like an agonizing hour of pain was really only a few minutes.

Her attackers were now out of breath but still gluttonous in their task. They dragged her motionless body under a group of nearby trees, out of sight from anyone. Charlotte lay in a pile of dirt and blood as the boys sat beside one another in a circle around her, analyzing what they had done and silently congratulating one another on the mayhem they had created. A few more minutes passed as they refueled themselves with flasks of alcohol and additional lines of drugs from one another's personal stashes.

The physical pain from the repeated blows was unbearable. The agony seemed to increase each time Charlotte blinked her eyes and she could feel her heart beating into every limb of her body. She was stunned from the continued assault and her body could not function. All Charlotte wanted to do was run but she was not able to move. The only movement came in random muscle flinches from the aftermath of the attack and this sent lightning rods of pain shooting throughout her body. She pleaded to herself:

"Just let them leave, please just let them leave."

But the terror had just started.

One of the lackeys straddled her by standing over her body and placed a foot onto each of her biceps, pinning her arms to the ground. He loomed over her with a grin that said:

"This is just the beginning."

Charlotte felt the other lackey slashing the bottom half of her clothes and also cutting away her blouse. Her shirt and skirt were both filleted by a knife and then torn from beneath her.

Charlotte now lay naked in this Hellish gruesome situation. She stared up at the sky in her outdoor prison of pain, fearing what she knew was going to come next. The dominant leader walked around her body to the top of her head, bent down, leaned in close to her right ear, and whispered:

"You are mine."

He then positioned himself on top of her and behind his accomplice that was still standing on her arms, preventing any kind of struggle. In every imaginable horrific way, he debased Charlotte to nothing and it did not stop. She tried to close her eyes but the goon standing on her arms repeatedly bent over to slap her in the face in order to keep her eyes open. The other lackey was laughing in hysterics and loving every moment of the assault. He circled the event and kept supplying liquor to his friends, pouring from a flask down each of their throats while they took part in the vicious attack. He came to the head of Charlotte and drenched her face with the liquor, searing the open gashes as if someone had lit them on fire.

This repeated until each of the assaulters had fulfilled himself. Charlotte lay motionless, writhing in mental anguish and physical pain and unable to fully comprehend the severity of what had just occurred. It was as if her life had been literally taken away and her mind was now a black hole full of pain and suffering.

The degenerates stepped back and admired their handiwork, scoffing at how pathetic their victim was. The dominant male of the group sputtered his next words:

"Let's destroy this waste."

He acquired a nearby rock that was sharply edged and heavy with size. Bending over Charlotte's body he swung hard, hitting the side of her head, which now split open from the force of the blow. Her world turned instantly black and she was motionless. The villains began to dress hastily but were interrupted as they saw the flashing of blue and red lights in the distance as well as the bobbing of several white flashlights that were quickly coming closer. Their greedy destruction had not gone unnoticed and each was tackled by a member of the NYPD who then threw them into the back of several police squad cars that had been alerted to the scene by a pedestrian who had witnessed the event.

An ambulance arrived at the horrific ordeal and paramedics began to test Charlotte for vital signs. It was clear that the case was dire. As she was rushed to the hospital Charlotte was able to summon one thought:

"Help me, my love."

Dave was waiting in their studio and at that moment felt something was wrong, terribly wrong. He paced the floor of the apartment and performed the standard checks when you worry about someone you love and cannot get a hold of them. Call their office and parents, both, of course, yielded no results. He knew she would be coming home right after work and if something had come up she would have notified him. The fact that he hadn't heard anything from her sounded a very serious internal alarm.

After repeatedly calling her phone for an hour it was finally answered. A female voice asked:

"Are you Dave Dougherty?"

"Yes I am, do you know where Charlotte is?"

"We do, please get down to the New York Presbyterian hospital at once. She has been attacked and is alive, but she is in a very poor and deteriorating condition."

There wasn't a single thought in Dave's mind except the desire to get to where Charlotte was. He left immediately and headed out the door. Dave quickly descended their steps and rushed out the front of the building and into the street. A cab pulled up and Dave rode in silence while his head swam in turmoil as the taxi made its way to the hospital.

Dave entered the hospital and approached the front desk where he was directed to a specific floor and then to a hallway where Charlotte's room was located. NYPD officers filled the space and instantly knew who he was upon seeing him due to the shocked questioning tumultuous look on his face. Dave attempted to shuffle past them but was stopped by an officer who requested identification. Once complete he was lead to another lead officer who began to brief him on the situation. A doctor also sided up to the group and stood quietly as the officer began to recount the dreadful situation. The detail was specific and Dave could feel his stomach tighten almost as if it had turned inside out with anguish. He began to visibly shake to the point where it was as if he would collapse. Two members of the police quickly stepped in to help support Dave and placed him into a nearby chair.

Now it was the Doctors turn. Dave held his head in his hands as the doctor began to speak:

"Please Dave, you have to look at me while I tell you this."

The doctor was crouched in front of him with one knee on the ground. Dave took his hands away from his face and revealed a pale expression, he was white with horror.

The doctor began to discuss the prognosis:

"So… I know, well I don't know how you feel at the moment but as horrific as the events that happened were, there is worse news. Her injuries are substantial and her life does not have much time left. I expect she will die from the injuries in less than 24 hours. There is nothing we can do."

"She is surprisingly lucid and has the ability to speak, however, her body is dying internally. I must tell you there is not a moment to delay. You need to get your wife's affairs in order immediately. I am so sorry, she is ready to see you now."

With that news, Dave stepped into Charlotte's hospital room.

Chapter 9

The Final Plan

Dave walked into the dimly lit room and up to Charlotte's bed. As he approached she noticed the movement and turned her head towards him and smiled that beautiful warm smile that he loved. He instantly burst into tears and delicately picked up her hand as he sat on the edge of the bed. There was an array of machines humming and beeping in the background with the purpose of sustaining her life. Their eyes met and Dave noticed she was also crying.

"Charlotte, they told me what happened and I know you are not okay."

She nodded in agreement and started to slowly speak:

"I just don't understand how this could happen to us. I have never harmed anyone or anything. We have struggled for so long in this worthless life and our place in the world has been meaningless and without hope. We never even wanted to be a part of this society, never had the desires of other people. All I ever wanted was to have peace and love but not just for myself, for everyone. I have been so unhappy with this life."

"Why did I have to be tortured at work by people I hated just to earn money for items we needed to survive? Why did I need to endure pain from my boss just so he could feel powerful?"

"And now this, how is my life over today like this? This life has been pointless and I never had a chance to explore any part of what I thought I was meant to do. We never even had the option because we didn't have enough money. We have always been tied down doing something we hated just so we could earn enough money to survive. Living by rules made by people who built a system that we don't agree with."

"This world just isn't right. Everyone is constantly fighting, killing, and not able to live together because of their different beliefs. But why?"

"Why can't we coexist in happiness with a common interest to help one another and live each day to the fullest?"

"This is what my life has come to, my life is over and it never even began."

"All I had was you. If it wasn't for our love I would have had no meaning in my life. Please go on living and don't spend another second doing something you hate. Please do this for me."

The tears flowed out of her eyes and she gasped:

"I love you."

Dave broke down and sobbed. She had said exactly what he also felt. Their connection in life had been brought together by their love. They were one shared existence and wanted to live for each other and instill that love and care into others. That was their purpose.

To Dave, nothing in this life mattered except for his love for Charlotte. A life without her did not need to exist and he would make that a reality.

He suddenly stopped crying as everything now became so clear. He couldn't go on without her and wouldn't. Without her he was nothing. Tears poured down Charlotte's face and Dave reached out, grabbing her hands in his.

"Charlotte, you won't be leaving me. Without you in my life I have nothing to live for, I will die with you."

"Dave no, you have to go on and change the way you live. You have to do something you love."

"Don't you see?" Dave proclaimed.

"There isn't anything else for me. This life was meant for only one thing, for us to be together. You know it and I know it, there is nothing fit for us in this world. Going to work and doing something we hate, seeing people kill one another on the news, and all done for things that have no meaning. You have felt it too, we just don't belong here. This sounds a little strange but my mind has never felt clearer in my entire life until now. I know what I was meant for and it is you. Without you, I don't want to be a part of this world. I love you and I will die with you."

"We don't have much time and I am going to set this life straight before we go."

"Dave, what are you going to do?"

"You know what I am going go to do."

Charlotte was quiet for a second, reading his thoughts with her eyes. She did know his plan.

"But you aren't supposed to die yet, just let me go."

"Never, and you know that I won't."

And Charlotte did know this and stopped fighting him. They would end their lives together.

"You will come back right?" Charlotte asked longingly.

"Of course. I'll be right back."

Dave bent over her head, kissed her goodbye, and left.

Chapter 10

Justice

Everything was clear. The future was set and Dave knew his path from now until death. There was nothing that clouded his thoughts.

All aspects and worries of common life that used to consume his daily thoughts were gone. All the rules of a system they never wanted to be a part of were now inconsequential. Love was the only rule that needed to be obeyed.

What else in the real meaning of existence mattered? The answer was nothing. Dave no longer feared death and knowing that the end was near alleviated all other uncertainties. He had no more concerns, just wrongs that needed to be righted.

Dave was a man on a ledge, capable of anything. Knowing your fate instills one with a feeling of confidence. An unwavering emotion to do what you know is right without the care of consequence.

It was to be a day of reckoning for the people that had

negatively affected their lives. Justice would be delivered in the most necessary of ways to these people that had corrupted their existence.

Chapter 11

The Checklist

The first stop for Dave would be their apartment to make the final arrangements. Preparing for these engagements was a bit harder than he expected for he was inexperienced with violence.

How do you go about physically hurting someone? What is the best tool to use? What do you wear? These items seemed easy in the movies but for someone with no familiarity, it was a challenge.

They had knives in the kitchen but could he actually stab someone? What else, ah yes, he had a very nice battery powered drill that was a gift from his father in law. Dave went to his closet, dusted off the case and pulled out the immaculate cordless drill. Pulling the trigger the drill hummed to life with a quick revolution and then abruptly stopped. Of course, in reality, a battery is always dead when you need it. The time it would take to charge the drill would be far too long and he quickly abandoned the plan.

Dave decided to let the events play out with no

preparation. He changed clothes into something pragmatic; athletic shoes, mesh black basketball workout shorts, and a well-fitting plain grey t-shirt. The only tools he deemed necessary on this final day was a debit card, driver's license, and a cellphone. As he turned to leave the apartment Dave took one last look at what they were leaving behind. Taking a quick inventory of their modest belongings he recognized a few sentimental items but really saw their loving home. A few seconds of detached deep thought brought him closure and that was that.

A very short future lay ahead, a future free of the system they had been a part of. It felt good to leave everything behind. It was a cleansing moment but full of regret that their life couldn't have lasted longer or had been lived differently. It was easier to make peace with it then he expected. Walking away from a material life was easy and it felt good to know that nothing other than his love for Charlotte mattered. The excess was what was worthless in the end. He turned and left their home behind, leaving the door to the apartment open.

Chapter 12

Judgment Part 1

The first part of the mission before death was to take a trip to his place of work. It was time to make a small difference in the world to a person that had wronged him by his revolting existence. Someone who was the opposite of what humanity should be, someone who needed to realize the right and wrong way to live, what was acceptable and what was not acceptable.

It was about half-past 8 AM when Dave hailed a cab and sped to the downtown office where most of his life was spent. Taking the elevator up to the office in his casual attire he arrived at the place of fraudulent business, the sales floor. Where everything he knew to be awful, however, today was different.

There was a steadfast feeling of certainty that Dave had never felt before. He was relaxed and sure of his intentions as he strode across the floor and into the kitchen. He helped himself to the coffee machine and poured a cup into a large heavy ceramic mug. Dave then began walking to the office of his boss and on the way, he received several questioning glances from his colleagues. He did not bother engaging anyone, the business at hand was more important.

He approached the glass wall of his boss's large extravagant office and pulled focus on his manager who was busy chatting away on an earpiece, laughing casually with his feet on the desk. Dave could overhear him narrating some pathetic weekend sexual conquest story but he stopped suddenly upon noticing Dave approaching. He shot Dave a quizzical glance while pointing to his expensive watch, which suggested that he was annoyed by Dave's tardiness. He could see Dave was about to open the door to his power office and quickly held up an index finger as a gesture to tell him to wait. On any other day, Dave would have given a respectful nod and scurried away about his usual business. However, today was unlike the past and there was only action to take. Dave burst through the door and strolled into the expansive office space with his coffee and walked right up to the boss's desk.

The quizzical look from the boss had quickly faded and had now turned into a smuggish smirk. He now desired to get off the phone so he could ask Dave what he was thinking. Barging in unexpectedly was not acceptable. The sales goon, still on the phone, swiveled in his chair to place his feet on the floor. Before he could Dave leaned over the desk towards the phone and clicked it dead with his right index finger.

Now the boss was clearly upset and his smug cocky look changed to disbelief and anger. His feet quickly planted on the floor with the intention of standing and yelling at his subordinate. Before he could transfer his weight to stand Dave threw the scalding coffee into his face. A shriek of pain and confusion sounded from the office and Dave's renewed sense of action left nothing to hesitation. Quickly, he moved around the desk and holding the cup by the handle, he thrashed the mug down upon the fake king's forehead. Raising the cup repeatedly over his head he then connected five separate times to the forehead of the boss as if hammering in a railroad tie with a sledgehammer.

A shocked and painfully stunned boss was now gasping for air and starting to cower in a confused state, but before he could move, Dave took his left hand and grabbed the end of the boss's tie. With one swift motion, he forcefully wrapped it around the neck of the monster like a tight lasso and then grasped the back of the boss's collar with the same hand. Dave now firmly held the tie and the back of the boss's shirt collar in his left hand. Dropping the coffee mug, which surprisingly had not broken, from his right hand he then seized the back of the belt and pants of the stunned boss. In half a second he ousted him out of his chair by the makeshift noose in his left hand and the tight hold of the pants in his right hand. Dave then dragged the boss across the floor to the glass wall of the office.

The boss's face was now pressed firmly on the glass in smooshed shivering contorted fear. Dave took a step back, dragging the boss back about 2 feet, and then quickly rushed forward, ramming the boss's head into his own glass wall. Still clutching the belt and shirt collar he pulled back and did it again and again. The office shook violently and the glass spidered. Again Dave stepped back but this time, instead of rushing immediately forward to the wall, Dave rapidly spun himself with the man-child 360 degrees counterclockwise, releasing the boss as the full circle was completed. This rocketed him like an Olympic hammer straight at the glass wall.

The body of the boss hit the glass straight up as if he was walking through it, shattering the wall in an incredible crash of force. The power of the throw shot his body across the hall causing him to ricochet off the opposing cubicle wall that was just outside of the office. He now lay flat on his back with shards of glass speckling his face. Hundreds of small puncture wounds were now running blood and it began to drip and flow down his cheeks. He lay completely motionless in shock and pain with heavily labored breathing. Dave gracefully stepped over him, straddling this pathetic quivering crying child of a man. He then lowered himself onto the boss's chest, kneeling down hard with his right knee, crushing the middle of his ribcage on the sternum. Dave drew close to his boss's face, their eyes met and Dave said:

"You are no better than anyone else."

Dave stood and turned to make his way to the elevator. From start to finish the whole ordeal took about thirty seconds. None of the other workers reached out to help their fallen battered leader for they too hated him and now reveled in his worthlessness. They looked on in shock but also with a silent form of gratitude, all wishing they could have done exactly the same thing.

As he left, Dave felt accomplished that some kind of world equilibrium had been set straight. In his past life, he would not have been able to complete this form of judgment. Only now when left with nothing, when the man-made rules of society did not matter, could this justice be done. Now off to the next item.

Chapter 13

Judgment Part 2

Dave hailed another cab and was off to Midtown East to pay a visit to Charlotte's boss. The tyrant that had so many times left her in tears and brought unneeded stress to both of their lives. Even more than just stress it had created a sickening stomach churning nervousness for her on a daily basis. This subhuman decided it was acceptable to take his own frustrations out on an innocent person by constantly belittling Charlotte and treating her as if she was an incompetent subservient human. Dave had been dealing with this for years and it pained him to see Charlotte so upset and unable to sleep. She was constantly checking her email day and night, fearing the wrath of what was to come the following day from her pathetic boss.

Well, his world was about to change. As the cab pulled up to the building Dave was glad to see that his bank was conveniently located on the nearby street corner. This office would not be quite as easy to get into as his own. The last day on Earth would require something that he hated so much and yet was forced to desire more of, money. It was ironic that even though life didn't actually need it, nothing could survive or be accomplished without it.

He entered the bank, handed over his ID to the teller and swiped his debit card at the window. Dave then requested a withdrawal of all of the cash they had, dropping their joint account down to zero. The usual thought when taking a withdrawal from the bank was a calculated one. Their budget did not have room for frivolous actions and a cash withdrawal always had a specific purpose. Today the withdrawal felt like a relief, $10,000. It was all the money they had to their name and had taken a decent amount of frugal behavior to accumulate. As the teller counted and distributed the bills onto the counter a smile crossed Dave's face.

How meaningless was this paper? Someone decided it would rule the world and it resulted in a life of torment for so many people. It caused them to do terrible atrocities just to get more of it.

Dave continued to smile while thinking that even on his last day on the planet he still needed it. In the past, this type of transaction would have caused severe anxiety but today it made him happy for he finally felt like he had always wanted to, free of money.

Dave didn't care about what happened to the money nor did he worry about how long it would take to replace it. This transaction provided a feeling of uncorrupted freedom and it felt amazing. No longer was he held down by the constraints of money and he only hoped that others could also someday share this liberating feeling. The teller finished counting out the bills and asked about the status of the now empty account. Dave gave a peaceful smile and turned without answering. No longer a slave to a system he didn't care about.

He entered Charlotte's office building and marched to the front desk while passing a garbage can to his right. He gently gave a simple drop of the debit card and driver's license into the round opening of the can. These items were no longer necessary in this life.

He approached the security desk and asked to go to the 60th floor.

“ID please sir,” the security guard asked.

Quietly and respectfully Dave replied:

“I actually don’t have my ID and I also don’t have an appointment. I am here to visit my wife’s boss. She is actually in the hospital and will not be with us much longer. There is a message I need to deliver to him, so if you could just let me up I would appreciate it.”

“Sir, I am sorry but I...”

Before she could finish the sentence Dave fanned out $5,000 and neatly slid it across the counter so she could easily see the amount. The security guard silently gave Dave a once over judgment and quickly came to the conclusion that he was no mass murderer or terrorist. She could sense his intentions were sincere and the $5,000 was enough to remove any hesitation from her decision. Dave couldn’t help his amusement. It was funny to think of how persuasive a quick sum of money could be. Without another glance, she extended her hand to take the money and at the same time, while looking the other way, printed and handed him a building pass that would scan at the turnstile to get him upstairs.

He rode to the top floor and extended the same $5,000 courtesy to the front desk receptionist who also gladly and quickly accepted the offer while directing Dave to the appropriate hall that would lead to the door of Charlotte’s boss.

Dave walked through the office without bringing much attention to himself. No one knew him here and his attire probably meant he was a bike messenger. He approached the office and saw Charlotte’s empty desk just outside of it. It was bare and lacked any emotion or character. This office was a dark void absent of anything good in the world. There was however a framed picture on the desk. It was of Charlotte and Dave on their wedding day. Her beaming radiant smile stopped Dave in his tracks and he stared at the image with tears immediately falling from both eyes. This office had brought her so much pain from a person incapable of knowing the right and wrong way to treat someone. A quick yell bellowed from the office of Charlotte's boss and quickly snapped Dave back to attention.

He flung open the door, which crashed into a coat rack and sent it falling loudly to the floor. The startled boss was standing a few yards behind his desk and looked visibly angry at being interrupted from the tirade he had been delivering to someone on the phone. He pulled the receiver away from his face in confusion.

"Do you know who I am?" Dave asked calmly.

"No, and you are disturbing me. And why would I care who you are? I can't find my assistant and if she was here she wouldn't have let you in, now get …"

Before he could finish the sentence Dave arrived at the front of the desk with one long swift stride. Upon arriving he reached out to the desk with both hands and grasped the right and left short sides of the boss's keyboard. He then placed his right foot on the top edge of the front of the desk for leverage and heaved the keyboard with enough quick force to snap it free from the cable attaching it to the computer. With the now free keyboard in both hands, he treated the desk like a box jump and landed squarely on top of it. Both feet were now planted firmly and Dave jumped straight off with the keyboard raised above his head like a battle-ax. He sailed through the air and connected the flat of the board directly onto the face of the standing boss. It violently broke in half and sent the keys exploding across the office in all directions. They both landed in a mound on the floor with Dave clutching the left side of the now broken keyboard in his right hand and found himself advantageously positioned on top of the boss. He adjusted his right handhold on the one half of the broken board by curling four fingers over the top of the flat end on the short side of the board. He then wrapped his thumb around the other side that was perpendicular to it. The flat of his palm now supported the underside of the board and Dave brought the severed broken jagged edge down like a heavy guillotine, hard and swift onto the boss's exposed neck. The sharp plastic edges savagely pierced his skin in multiple areas and the force of the blow caused him to choke and desperately wheeze for air. His hands went to his throat and he was able to see light faint streams of blood trickling down his fingers.

Dave stood and watched the boss clutch his neck and awkwardly scoot his cowering hunched form to the corner of his office by frantically pushing his feet away from himself while still on the floor. His eyes were wide with terror and when he reached the corner he began to curl himself into a protective ball with his back against the wall. Dave positioned himself on the left end of the boss's desk and swiveled it so the right side faced the boss. He then flung the left side up so the desk now stood on its right end, vertically upright. With a strong quick push, Dave sent the desk toppling over and the flat top of the heavy desk landed right on the boss's head, crumpling his whole body underneath it. A wailing high pitched scream was heard as Dave then heaved the desk off to reveal a shuddering sobbing, blood-spattered shell of a man that what was once a power wielding individual.

"I am Dave Dougherty, the husband of your assistant you worthless pathetic waste of humanity. At what point in your disgusting existence did you think it was okay to treat my wife the way that you did? I have watched her suffer from the pain and anxiety that you caused and could not stand the thought of knowing you existed in our life. Well, look at you now you arrogant piece of trash. Enjoy the rest of your day, you subhuman unnecessary form of life."

Dave then turned back to the desk, tore out a thick dense drawer and raised it above his head. The drawer, still filled with the contents it possessed, was then swung down onto the head of the brute, splintering and cracking upon connecting. The contents of the drawer erupted and fell all around the scene. A weak defeated whimper emerged from the boss as he crumpled into a fetal position on the floor. This process had taken a little longer than the first and totaled about two minutes from start to finish. In no way were the injuries life-threatening but they would leave their mark. As Dave left the office down the same way he came in he noticed that no one spoke to him and that there was a stunning similarity from the events that happened in his own office. The workers crowded around their fallen dictator in shock and awe at what had happened but did not offer to help. They too wanted him destroyed and basked in the victory. What an interesting pattern from workplace to workplace. Dave left feeling fulfilled. There was now one more task to complete.

Chapter 14

Judgment Part 3

The satisfaction of degrading two people that had affected their lives in such a negative way was very rewarding. The two individuals had been physically hurt and he did not feel bad about it at all. There was no other way to get through to such arrogant people. Dave could only hope that the impression he made on each of them would change the way they treated people in the future. It was a necessary balance in life that needed to be restored and it would hopefully bring them back to equilibrium with the rest of society. No one should be permitted to treat anyone in a way that they would not like to be treated. Arrogance has no place in life and if Dave only had one last day to live he would be sure to end it by setting something right in the world.

The last piece was to seek revenge on Charlotte's assailants. It was a simple decision. They had killed her and this had taken away his meaning to live. They did not deserve to be alive and could no longer be a part of humanity.

Finding them, now how could this be done? Dave decided to call the hospital.

"Hello, this is officer... Jones, uh, calling about Charlotte, the lady in critical care that was assaulted last night. We are bringing the three suspected attackers back to the hospital for more blood work. Time is critical here and we may need Charlotte to identify them. Quickly, which police department did the other officers take the attackers to?"

The receptionist hesitated.

"Officer, we have been given strict orders to not reveal any information regarding the..."

She was cut short by Dave's interruption.

"Miss, she will die today. I am on the case and can't get ahold of the other police officers at the hospital, please hurry."

"Well, they have all actually been released to one of the boy's fathers and are currently under house arrest at his residence. All three are at the same location. Apparently, one of the attacker's fathers is some big shot lawyer in the city and was able to get them out of jail."

"Miss, thank you. Now please, what is the address?"

"Yes of course," and she quickly gave the address of the attacker's Upper Eastside location.

"Thank you," Dave said and hung up the phone.

With the location complete Dave began a brisk walk of purpose to the residence. He was calm and came to the conclusion that he did not know how the next step would play out. Dave had no knowledge of how to operate this way but that thought was fleeting. He would just simply take care of it. As he came upon the residence he passed a trashcan and threw the cellphone in an underhanded nonchalant toss. There was no longer a need for this final possession.

Looking up at the house it struck him as an enormous ostentatious structure. The immensely grand brownstone was clearly the living place of a multimillionaire. The impressive structure had one police officer and another stout man wearing a suit standing out front. It appeared that these two were guarding the entrance.

How could he get inside? Dave's natural reaction told him to keep matters simple and he climbed the steps of the house, meeting the guards at the door.

"Gentlemen my name is Dave and I am Charlotte's husband. I am sure you are aware of the circumstances surrounding her and you must be aware that she will die today. I am here to see to it that the responsible parties cease to exist."

Humbly and calmly Dave delivered this message. The three of them stood in silence as the two sentries made eye contact with one another. As if coming to an unspoken agreement the police officer began to speak without looking at Dave.

"You must enter through the butler's quarters to the left of this staircase. Go straight back down the hallway which will lead you to a kitchen. You will see a door that leads to the backyard of the house and you will then see a patio. The fire escape steps at the patio will lead you to the back door of the main house's kitchen. All three of the people you are looking for are inside."

It was recited as if prepared and both men showed no expression at all. It was as if they had been told to deliver the message. Dave hesitated for a moment as he digested the delivery of this information. He couldn't help but think that there was some type of outside influence in this situation. Time was of the essence and he chose to not give it any additional thought. He turned to descend the steps and the two guards began talking again as if they had never seen him. Very odd Dave thought, but if fate would have it this way then who was he to spend another second questioning its simplicity.

As a matter of fact, fate was present at that moment. An invisible Angel had been there the entire time, influencing the guards. The same way that God had influenced all of the events leading up to this point.

Dave followed the instructions. He entered the butler's quarters and then moved through the hallway to the backyard. He then lively ascended the fire escape and entered the unlocked back door to the house. There was loud electronic techno music blaring from inside and he could see shadows of movement coming from a dimly lit room ahead through a small hallway that led away from the kitchen. The impeccable kitchen was gigantic and resembled something from an architecture magazine. Walking quickly through the kitchen, Dave briefly paused and reached up with his right hand to unhook a thick, dense, well-made copper frying pan from a variety of expensive cooking ware that hung above the granite-topped counter of the kitchen's island. There was a block of knives to his immediate left and he withdrew one, yielding a medium sized paring knife. It was light and small but the blade was strong and had the sturdiness of fine craftsmanship.

Dave walked silently to the end of the hall and carefully peered around the corner and saw the three killers in a dimly lit expansive studious space that resembled the Rose Reading Room at the New York Public Library. One of them was seated at a massively thick wooden table surrounded by bottles of liquor. Another one was standing just to the right of him holding a bottle of alcohol in one hand and thrusting his other hand into the air to the beat of the painfully loud techno music. The last one was standing on the right side of the table closest to Dave, his body hunched over a pile of white powder.

This was some kind of celebration that they were partaking in. Clearly, they were toasting their victory of making bail that was handed to them by one of their well-connected parents. Dave had passed a number of photos while walking through the hallway. One of those photos was of a young man who Dave recognized as the person sitting at the table in this room. He seemed to be the ringleader of the three and it must have been his father who was the powerful New York lawyer for this room was filled with several plaques and framed degrees representing various legal awards and credentials. Of course, these privileged individuals were able to use the influence of their family to their benefit. This group of scum would never be brought to proper justice since the power of their family clearly had the ability to sway a system of corrupt civil servants. This was the culminating factor that ignited a fire of rage within Dave. They would see justice and he would give it to them.

Dave sprinted to the closest attacker who was still hunched over the table. Wielding the copper pan like a club he bashed the back of the attackers head with it. The blow was hard and sent the boy's face directly into the surface of the table. The youth's nose connected with a shattering fracturing thud. The powder he was snorting exploded in a white cloud and his head bounced back up as he fell backward to the floor.

The other boys sprang up in surprise and froze. Dave picked up the victim by the back of his collar and steadied him onto his feet, holding him up from behind. This revealed the grotesque outcome of his face. It seemed to have changed shape after meeting the table and blood was profusely gushing from his nose, covering his face, neck, and shirt. The blood had mixed with the powder and was now caked on his face in a crimson type of violent batter. This startling sight continued to freeze the other two and Dave shouted:

"Music off!"

The standing killer shook himself from his startled pose and picked up a nearby remote from the table, quickly turning off the sound. There was a moment of silence that was broken by Dave's new prisoner who began to sputter blood as he attempted to breathe.

Dave addressed the two individuals who were free from

his grasp, pointing at the one who had turned the music off.

"You, duct tape now."

"Please, wait, let's..."

But he was cut off as Dave's left arm curled swiftly upwards in an instant to the top of his captive's left shoulder. The knife was in his hand and it plunged into the boy's flesh all the way up to the handle in one immediate motion. The speed of the brutal act left the other two with the same thought:

"Don't ask questions, just do as you're told."

The afflicted victim that Dave was still holding let out a high-pitched scream, adding a level of seriousness to this no-nonsense situation.

The youth took the order from Dave, dropped his bottle of liquor and sprang to the kitchen. The noise of a panic-stricken individual clambering through drawers and cupboards was apparent but before ten seconds had passed he returned with a full roll of duct tape. Dave crossed the floor, dragging his bleeding victim to the other two, and shoved the accomplice towards them. Without Dave to steady his balance, he lost his footing and crashed to the ground.

Dave addressed his new tape-wielding servant:

"You, tape the hands and feet of the other two."

Sloppily and hastily the scared piece of human trash began to do what he was told. He rendered each of his friends fairly immobile and they were now laying flat on their stomachs.

"Now lie down and hand me the tape."

He did as he was told and Dave began a much more secure and very restrictive taping process. He roughly passed the roll around the shaking limbs of the body so tightly that it immediately started cutting off the attacker's circulation. Dave repeated this process with the other two until all three were completely immobile, side-by-side, with bellies down, and feet facing towards him. He took a step back to evaluate his handiwork and gave a snorting exhale and nod of approval, confident that they were stationary.

He then named them. Fitting titles would be lackey one (the one who received the stab wound and who was profusely bleeding from his nose), lackey two (tape boy), and then the ringleader.

Approaching both lackeys, Dave kneeled, took a firm hold of each of their heads of hair, and dragged the both of them to the edge of the room away from the table. He flipped each over like a bag of dirt and propped them up in a sitting position against the sidewall to the right of the table. The same action was then performed to the ringleader. Dave stepped back again to take a look and was visibly pleased with the sight before him. Here they were, the three people that had done the unspeakable to his loving and peaceful wife, ultimately killing her and bringing an end to his own.

They were bound before him and uncomfortably restricted, all sitting shoulder to shoulder. Dave let the silence do the talking and the severity of the situation began to soak into the brains of the group as they evaluated their circumstances. The ringleader surprisingly still had an air of entitlement and arrogance. In a smug confident tone, the ringleader spoke:

"Look, I don't know who you think you are but I would run right now if I were you. My father has this house locked down and we are protected. If you leave now I won't say anything but if you stay, you are going to jail for a long time. I doubt you know of my family but we are powerful in this city and will make your life very unpleasant."

Dave silently stared back at the ringleader. Their eyes held and Dave gave a quick judgmental tight-lipped smile accompanied with a long blink of his eyes.

Stepping forward Dave raised the copper pan, which was in his right hand, and brought the bottom of it down hard across the left side of the ringleader's face as if the pan was an extension of his own arm. It was the equivalent of slapping someone in the face but with a very heavy piece of metal instead of a hand. The blow whipped the ringleader’s head to the right and Dave’s hand that held the pan followed through and paused high over his own head after delivering the blow. His right arm had crossed his upper torso and with the pan now hovering over his left shoulder he flipped the pan so the bottom faced outward. Dave then brought down another blow, backhanding the ringleader with the hard metal and snapping his head back in the opposite direction. The force of these two strong blows ripped into the ringleader’s head and before his thoughts could begin to take shape Dave stepped backward and a bit to the left. Taking a baseball batter's stance he clutched the pan as if he was taking a pitch and swung like he was hitting a home run. The flat side of the pan crushed the front of ringleader’s face and blood instantly ejected from his nose as he wailed helplessly in pain.

Fear overcame lackey two after seeing this quick act of violence and he let out a scream. Dave sidestepped to the right and brought the flat side of the pan diagonally across the right and left sides of the lackey’s face. These blows squarely bashed each side of the lackey’s nose and now he too was profusely bleeding.

Dave stepped back again to admire his work. All three of his victims were in terrible shape, heavily battered, and were starting to swell and bleed all over themselves. It was a grotesque sight. Lackey three had been quiet since his initial beating and now began to wet his pants in fear. Silence from Dave continued as the three captives wheezed heavily and spat blood on the floor as they tried to gather their bearings.

Now it was Dave’s turn for smugness and he addressed the ringleader:

“I believe you mentioned something about unpleasantness. Did you feel what just happened to you? Do you see the blood that is spilling down your face?”

"Hhm," Dave scuffed.

"What a ridiculous question, of course you see the blood. Please, tell me, how do you feel right now? Do you feel powerful? Do you feel or sense that someone is going to save you?"

Dave waited for a response in silence after delivering this message.

"Well, no one, no one has an answer? How very interesting. Well, let me continue. You may suspect who I am by now. I am the husband of the lady you decided to assault, ultimately killing her, and taking her away from me. Now, allow me to tell you what I am going to take from you. Please pay attention."

Dave began to point to each of them with the frying pan.

"I will kill lackey one first and I will have both of you watch. Then I will kill lackey two and you will just watch Mr. ringleader. I mean obviously, lackey one won't be able to watch because he will be dead."

Dave nodded his head while glancing at all three as if he was looking for some type of approval regarding the future events.

"Then I will kill you Mr. ringleader and you will only see me as you die. I have never done this before so hopefully it goes smoothly. Please prepare yourselves, seriously. There is no time to waste for you will all three be dead very shortly. These are the last minutes of your life. Please, feel free to take some time to evaluate this."

Dave stood back after delivering this message. The two lackeys cried out, blubbering desperate forms of apologies. They cried and sobbed but the ringleader still managed to keep his arrogance.

"You can't do this and will never get away with it," he stammered through a mouthful of blood.

Dave walked to lackey one and pulled him away from the group, turning him to face his accomplices. He then began wrapping layer upon layer of duct tape around the bottom half of his head until his nose and mouth were completely covered by the tape. It formed an airtight seal and the bottom half of his head looked like a grey mask. His panicked breathing became labored in a matter of seconds as Dave lowered himself onto his knees and with his right arm formed a chokehold around the lackey's neck. With his left hand, he pulled back and held the front of the lackey's hair so he could control his head, forcing the lackey's eyes to be level with the ringleader and lackey two.

The choking boy's outstretched taped legs began to thrash as he was overcome with the desire to breathe. The other two were now screaming at the sight of his pending death. The eyes of the attackers darted back and forth between each other and slowly the legs of lackey one began to not move as much. It almost seemed like he was going to sleep in Dave's iron grip chokehold and then, he ceased to move at all.

The other two killers stared in disbelief as Dave continued to choke him even though he was no longer moving. They began crying uncontrollably, now fully understanding that no assistance was coming. They felt helpless for the first time in their lives. All of their privilege, power, and money was starting to feel worthless as they knew their lives were coming to an end.

Dave dragged the now dead lackey to the side of the room by his legs and came back to crouch in front of the remaining two.

"Hmm," Dave muttered calmly, giving both a sarcastic questioning look.

Dave pointed at the ringleader.

"Did you see what just happened? Now you mentioned I, wait.., what was it that you said? Ah yes, you said I can't do this."

"Well as you can see…" Dave gave a wide gesture with his arm to the deceased.

"Yes, I can."

"Now as I said before, there is a second part to this. Let

us repeat."

And the identical process happened with the ringleader unable to look away. Dave was crouched in a chokehold again, directly in front of the ringleader with his face right next to lackey two, cheek to cheek. Dave fiercely stared into the ringleader's eyes while his shot back and forth in desperate panic as he watched his friend die in front of him. The event unfolded exactly as before and the motionless deceased was dragged and heaped over the other.

"Do you see what I have done here? Hah, another silly question, of course you do. You see, I will also die today."

"That is why I do not care about anything that you may think is important. I have taken the fundamentals of society and literally thrown them away. There is no amount of power and no amount of money that can save you. These things are meaningless to me and as you can see, also meaningless in your case as well. I only had love in my life and you took it away from me. Since I cannot go on living I decided that your life needed to end as well. These are the consequences for your actions."

The ringleader's world came crashing down in a second. Knowing his life was over he turned away from Dave, unable to look at him. Gently, Dave kneeled before him and lightly turned his face towards his own.

"I am the last person you will ever see. Are you ready?"

The ringleader began to violently shake.

"No please no," he wailed and Dave began to mask his face, leaving him struggling to breathe like the others.

Dave laid him on his back and straddled him. One hand covered the ringleader's nose and the other hand covered his mouth. Dave was sitting on his chest right up to his neck and squeezing the sides of the ringleader's head between his knees. Dave stared silently into the killer's eyes with a determined cold unwavering glare. The eyes of the ringleader were wide and horrified. They began to blink longer and longer and he began to thrash less and less. It was over.

Dave walked back to the kitchen, happy, relieved, and justified. He was not pleased to kill but there was no other way. Peace was all he wanted but this world would not allow it. This life had failed him and Charlotte and he was glad to be leaving a world where they did not belong.

He rushed back to the hospital. The police and doctors cleared away as they saw him run down the hallway towards Charlotte's room. One of the doctors put a hand on Dave's shoulder.

"It will only be minutes now," the doctor said. Dave then entered her room.

Chapter 15

The End of Love

Warm tears streamed down Dave's face as he entered the dark room. Charlotte, lying on her back, turned to him and gave a slow smile. He nodded to her in return. She knew it was done. As he approached the bed he could see she was is in a labored state and he grasped her feeble hands with both of his. She was dying right before his eyes. He leaned over her and his tears began falling on her face, quickly he brushed them away with his hand.

"Don't go Charlotte, please don't leave me."

Charlotte began to cry as well and in a tight frightful breathless voice, she said her last words:

"I'm scared and I don't want to die. I feel so lost and afraid."

"Dave… I love you, please stay with me, please don't let me die, stay with me."

And then she was gone, dead, her eyes wide open. Dave leaned down and drew in her last breath. He then climbed on top of the bed knowing that he had no reason to live, retrieved the paring knife he took from the house and slit his own throat.

On top of his love, cradling her head, caressing her hair, staring into those beautiful grey stormy sea eyes, he began to drift away. He bent down to meet her forehead with his and then Dave also died.

He died looking only at her. The only thing he ever really saw and ever truly loved.

Chapter 16

The Decision

God spoke to the Angels and to Lucifer as the two souls made their way to their respected afterlife destinations:

“It is done and they will now decide.”

“Lucifer, go to your Hell and give Dave the knowledge of our existence and I will do the same to Charlotte. Upon them knowing the choice they need to make we will then bring them together here in my kingdom to decide.”

Lucifer left Heaven and both souls arrived in the afterlife. Dave in Hell for ending his God-given life and Charlotte in Heaven for not having a choice regarding her own.

As they both became aware of their surroundings they felt an overwhelming feeling of relief. Finally knowing that there was more to existence was pure happiness and both were overjoyed, momentarily.

Chapter 17

Hell is Revealed

Lucifer met Dave in Hell's warm beautiful embrace and Dave felt at peace in what he saw. Hell looked like Earth and he could sense the love and harmony that it represented.

Lucifer spoke to Dave:

"What you see before you is Hell, a mirror image of Earth that is absent of the atrocities that plague the planet today. I created the Earth to be a place of peace and harmony where living beings could exist together in a tranquil, loving, and harmonious existence. I made this for God as a gift of originality that was meant to prove my devotion and love."

"God was jealous of my ingenuity and thought my creation was a challenge. God, the original creator, could not stand to have a perfect world exist that was created by another being. This jealousy caused God to devise a plan to destroy the Earth and all life on it."

"To execute this plan God needed to create a controllable form of life, humans."

"Humans were formed out of the blood of the Angels.

Since humans are literally a part of the Angels that meant they were essentially a part of God because God created them as well. That connection gives God and the Angels the ability to manipulate and control humanity."

"God then assigned the Angels to the different groups of humanity and ingrained specific religious beliefs into each human faction. The Angels then had the task of influencing all of their decisions."

"Everything you have seen happen, everything you were never able to understand; religion, faith, war, killing, the struggle for power, the lust for money, and the destruction of the Earth. That was all the work of God and the Angels. They have influenced every human action and thought in order to destroy the beautiful planet for their own glory. The Heavens forced humanity to be a part of this demented game of life and your species has acted as a pawn, living a controlled existence from birth only to be God's tool of obliteration."

"I could no longer accept the destruction of Earth and asked God to be forgiven. I wanted to be removed from existence so I no longer had to witness the annihilation of the beautiful planet and the lives on it. Instead of granting my request God chose to let me live, forcing me to watch the demise of life outside of Heaven."

"I could not bear to see this happen and decided to challenge God, to end this mayhem, and God accepted it."

"We agreed to create true love. A love absent of Heaven's influence that would decide the fate of existence. This is why you felt like you didn't belong in the world."

"God built the love you both share by setting a path in motion for you two to endure several predestined events. These planned events developed and strengthened your relationship and ultimately resulted in your death, which revealed the true love that you both shared. A love so pure that nothing else mattered, not even your own life."

"This true love that you have for each other will naturally

give you the desire to be together for eternity in the same place, Heaven or Hell. Once each of you is given the knowledge of Heaven and Hell you will then be brought together to decide which existence you want to live in."

"Look before you at the life in Hell."

"It is a peaceful place of love and harmony for the souls that God considered unfit to enter Heaven. The only souls allowed in Heaven are the ones that worshiped God unconditionally and without doubt. These souls do not exist in Heaven as equals, instead, they are enslaved to build God's always expanding kingdom for eternity with no memory of their previous life on Earth."

"If you and Charlotte choose Hell as your final resting place then all the souls in existence will be released to this domain. They will regain the knowledge of their past lives and be reunited with their loved ones to live in peace for the rest of time."

"If you choose Heaven every soul will also be reunited but will be part of God's kingdom and exist as slaves, forced to build God's empire forever."

"Your love is the truest form in existence and now you can choose to exist forever with Charlotte in peace, in Hell. A free existence to live together for eternity and reunite all the souls ever created. They will all worship you and you will be able to rule these beings for the rest of existence in the pure and harmonious way of life that you believe in."

"A life in Hell must be your choice."

Chapter 18

Heaven is Revealed

In Heaven, Charlotte had been summoned to sit next to God on the throne to observe Lucifer's explanation of Hell to Dave. She now understood what life in Hell meant.

God spoke to Charlotte as Dave and Lucifer witnessed her enlightenment from their place in Hell:

"As you can see I have created everything. All that lives, all that you have, was made by me. Lucifer's only contribution was a flawed world without the purity of what this existence really is. It cannot exist without a ruler. The souls of existence need to know and worship their creator in order to have a purpose. In Heaven we will exist, Hell will be no more, and the true order of life shall be restored. You and Dave will rule with me and together we will be the Gods of all matter of life. You will be worshiped like me and be able to mold the Heavens in any way that you please. Both of you will have the gift of creation and by doing so all will love and worship you as well. A truly meaningful existence can only be achieved in Heaven."

"What you see before you is flawless. A glistening paradise of perfection where I am the all-powerful creator and loved by all the members of Heaven."

"Heaven is creation and we are tasked with testing the souls of Earth to bring about only the best in them so they can be a part of my kingdom."

"This can be your only choice, rule as a God with me."

God ultimately controlled everything and knew Heaven would be the choice.

They both had the knowledge of the two eternal realms and a decision had to be made. Dave was brought to Heaven and he now stood with Charlotte on the floor of God's kingdom. Lucifer, the Disciples, and the mob of Angels were all assembled in the stands of the coliseum, looking down at the two who would decide the fate of existence.

Charlotte and Dave looked at each other in the afterlife and smiled. Surprisingly they did not feel the weight of the world on their shoulders. They were just happy, happy to be together and to know that finally, they could exist forever in love. Their love was all that mattered and it was true, existing without the influence of the Heavens. A smile crept upon both of their faces as Charlotte nodded to Dave in a silent acknowledgment of agreement. She knew what he thought and he knew what she thought. The decision was made.

Dave spoke to God:

"The lives of Earth are not your pawns of destruction."

"We have been manipulated since being created and have existed strictly for your constant lust for power. You have forced us to live in a constant state of torment since we were never allowed to know the future of our life after death. If you would have stopped your game of power and just showed us, told us there was an afterlife then the world would have been a different place."

"If humanity had been given the choice to just live, free of Heaven's control then humans would not be the people they are today. We would have chosen a life of peace if you would have allowed us to see that there was something else beyond our life on Earth. You forced us to desire money and power which was really only meant to destroy our shared planet."

"And now you have built a love that tortured two innocent souls just to prove that you are the master of existence?"

"We choose neither Heaven or Hell. Existence will have no ruler, only free eternal peace for every soul."

This choice was not expected and Heaven was unable to process the outcome. The silence was broken by the thunder of God's wrath. The creator of existence sent a torrent of lightning from the sky, striking the floor of Heaven where Charlotte and Dave stood until it glowed white with ferocious heat.

"You will choose!" God boomed to the universe.

"I am your creator and you have no choice but to choose one or the other!"

Dave confidently addressed God:

"We will never choose to be a part of either domain. We never wanted to rule anything and receiving your love is meaningless to us."

God had a solution to their unexpected response and the challenge would now end. God controlled everything and decided Dave and Charlotte would no longer have the ability to choose. God would silence them with the one thing that mattered most, love.

"I made your love and I can also take it away."

And God then took away their true love.

Chapter 19

True Love Survives

God tried to take away true love, but could not.

God had mistakenly created pure love in the first humans that did not carry the blood of the Angels in their bodies. Upon the creation of true love, the blood of the Angels was naturally expelled from both the bodies of Charlotte and Dave, unbeknownst to God. In God's arrogance to win Lucifer's challenge, God neglected to realize that by creating true love between two humans it literally meant they would exist as two independent beings. They were absent of all matter of Heavenly influence or control. God was able to control all of the surrounding events that eventually led to the death of Charlotte and Dave but was unable to control their own thoughts and actions directly. The blood of the Angels, made by God, is what controlled the humans. Without that present in their bodies, God had no ultimate power over them and so could not take away their love.

To have true love is to have pure devotion for another, absent of all other desires. The love Charlotte and Dave possessed was so powerful that it canceled out the human need for power and the lust for money. These common trappings of humanity meant nothing to them. When offered the ability to have the power to rule Heaven or Hell they both could not comprehend ruling any form of life and therefore had no longing to be a part of either domain. They only wanted life to be a true harmonious equal loving existence.

God's creation had backfired with the design of their love. They were the first of their kind, uncontrollable independent living beings. The true love that God created allowed them the freedom to not desire anything else.

God had been the single piece of perfection in existence. The creation of true perfect uncontrollable love defied the very essence of God. Since nothing could control God, nothing could also control perfection created by God. If God made an equal, true love, then God could not have any power over it.

This was a mistake and a God cannot make a mistake. God had disproved what it meant to be a God through perfection, which revealed that nothing is perfect. Everything is flawed in a perfect way.

Charlotte and Dave both realized their love remained and upon this realization, Dave spoke to God:

"Believe and have faith in this, you are not a God."

Immediately the Disciples, the mob of Angels, and God ceased to exist. The boundary between Heaven and Hell was instantly gone and it was now one afterlife for all to exist in for eternity. The souls of both domains were suddenly released. They regained the knowledge of their past and were instantly reunited with their loved ones.

Hell had now become the true existence and supported the way life should be, free. Free to love and to live in harmony without control. Lucifer knew that it had been wrong to compete with God for the control of existence. Life on Earth and life after Earth needed to be completely free. At that moment Lucifer decided that any Angel built from God would always desire a form of power and that could not exist. The last Angel, Lucifer, no longer controlled by God, was then self-expelled from existence. Leaving all life to be free.

Chapter 20

Genesis

In the beginning, the beginning of real life without the rule of God, there was no Heaven or Hell, just an afterlife.

A world absent of God naturally flourished since all knew that there was life after death. Without the burden of questioning fate, all life could now live together in peace. There was no religion, power, or money. Life was now a beautiful coexistence to be enjoyed to the fullest every day by all living beings. It was a naturally balanced existence that supported a common understanding of a shared unity of life. This understanding eliminated the previous desires of greed and control and all matter of life lived side by side in peace.

The meaning of life had also been revealed. Life is meant to find, give, and cherish love.

Love then gave way to humanity's destiny. It is the destiny of humanity to help all matter of life and to make a difference to our shared home of Earth.

Love is the very foundation of life and it is what solved

our existence.

The overwhelming happiness of a peaceful way of life was felt each day and all knew that true love did exist and that in the end it really does conquer all.

The End

Or…

Could it be that the purpose of God was to push the world to the brink of annihilation in order for its inhabitants to realize the true meaning of life, which is love? Maybe God had given humanity a parting gift. The gift to now create love in a peaceful world absent of all control.

Perhaps God still existed and went on to create light again in a new world, for there will always be another beginning.

The End

I love you Cake.

ABOUT THE AUTHOR

Nick Girard lives with his wife, Lisa Timbers, and their cat, Patches, in Boca Raton, FL.